WHEN THE DEAD WALK

An Original Horror Novel

by

Gary Lovisi

RAMBLE HOUSE

2014

First published in 2014 by

Ramble House
10329 Sheephead Drive
Vancleave MS 39565 USA

First Edition

© 2014 Gary Lovisi

Cover Art © 2014 Ed Coutts

Interior illustrations & design © 2014 Gavin L. O'Keefe

Edited by Gary Lovisi and Fender Tucker

ISBN 13: 978-1-60543-767-5

CONTENTS

Chapter 1: The Mansion

 **HEY** SAY THERE ARE GHOSTS in LaRontue Mansion. Grim dark things not of this world. The long-lost souls of far away inhabitants who have never fit into these modern times. These are the outcasts, the old, useless dregs of a society that seeks constant youth, a precarious renewal at the expense of the accumulated knowledge and valuable experience of far older and wiser heads.

Dead men in cold dark graves, lying in eternal wait.

Some will wait no longer!

These are some of the hauntings that ramble through those lonely old halls in the ill hours of the night, times of darkness and mystery when most decent people are safely tucked into their warm beds dreaming sweet dreams of love and wealth.

No such thoughts were capable of entering the shattered mind of Amos LaRontue, as his long, boney fingers clawed the damp earth that surrounded him; as his frenzied hands grabbed fistfuls of the harsh detritus in a never ending struggle outward and upward into the land of the living.

The man—or what was left of him—had been dead all these long months, buried in a shallow grave out behind the walled garden of LaRontue Mansion, the recipient of brother Lamont LaRontue's attack of insane jealously over the sexual attentions of the village girl, Alice Carmody.

That had all occurred in the dim past, in what was left of his dark, fetid memories. While it had been bare months ago, it was now a space of time that flowed into an era which no longer existed in the moldy vestiges of dim consciousness now awakening in the once formidable mind of Amos LaRontue. Now all that existed was a cold and thirsty primal hunger for revenge, and the vessel of that revenge was at hand with the appearance of the gypsy witch-woman, Sabella.

Sabella was dark and furtive, having recently been of alluring beauty, now grown suddenly grim and ugly in her desires to invoke black magic for hatred and revenge. She had powers but the use of them had twisted her, aged her immensely, so that the once lovely youthful woman she had once been, now had become an old withered crone. Nevertheless, she no longer cared about mere physical beauty, for now she possessed dark and mysterious powers, secrets that could not be explained by modern methods of science or logic. There were whispers uttered in dark quarters and the strangest of places about this woman—and in the past the name of Lamont LaRontue had been linked with hers in these dark stories as well. They would be once more.

These stories were scant and nebulous things, hints of black magic, animal sacrifice, potions of mysterious power and purpose. Sometimes worse. All in all, a woman whose reputation had preceded her to the dark halls of LaRontue Mansion and into the voracious arms of her once-lover, Lamont LaRontue.

None of this was of any consequence to the cold corpse that had once been Amos LaRontue as it continued to slowly dig itself upward from the fetid earth to escape its cold grave and bring itself into the stagnant warmth of the humid Louisiana summer night.

The last precarious dregs of memory remaining in this dead corpus had now been reawakened. Primal thoughts of terrible revenge and murder, made all so potent by the mysterious gypsy woman, who had made this nocturnal awakening possible by her mysterious manipulations of the magical equilibrium existing within the laws of nature.

The rictus of the dead thing smiled grotesquely, rotted teeth blackened to the gums, desiccated flesh hanging in casual patches, worms digging incessantly within the body like zealous playground children. The hot Louisiana air and moist soil had caused deep decay to what was left of the mortal remains of the murdered brother, but the body still somehow held together as a reanimated corpse that was able to move and walk and, soon, to kill. The thing that had once been Amos LaRontue slowly stood up and began walking in a lumbering gait towards the magnificence of LaRontue Mansion where brother Lamont was once more taking Alice Carmody to bed.

His beloved Alice!

The shutters held fast on the windows, flickering lights and low groans of male pleasure interspersed with female cries of passion and hunger came to the ears of the dead thing as it drew near. It knew not of these cries but somewhere deep within some dark vestiges of memory stirred. Slowly, and with the calm deliberation of one whose time is standing still within the eternity of death,

Amos LaRontue placed one moldy foot after the other upon the old creaking steps and entered the huge white columned porch of the stately Southern mansion that had once been his home.

From inside, there was the sound of low moaning from the lovers in the second bedroom as the thing approached, drawing ever nearer, dragging its lifeless remains closer and closer to the impassioned couple.

Meanwhile, in the bushes outside the house, overlooking the porch of the great mansion, stood the witch-woman, Sabella. Her long thin fingers plying their macabre trade with strange and utterly bizarre movements and devilish gestures not meant to be seen by the eyes of men. Movements and gestures that now were mysteriously mirrored in the animated corpse of Amos LaRontue as the dead thing approached the door and entered the elegant home. Like some marionette being manipulated by magical strings, Sabella controlled the shambling dead thing, causing it to move, to walk, to do what she willed it to do. She was in control and now she would use this walking dead thing she had created to seek her all-consuming hatred and revenge.

"And to think, you spurned my sweet caresses for this village slut, Lamont!" Sabella muttered in a menacing hiss. "Well, so be it!" The gypsy woman whispered with fire in her deep cold eyes. "Enjoy your fling with the young flesh of the servant girl—though God should save her from your terrible pleasures—and in a brief moment, from my own more terrible revenge. For at this very moment a grim and ghastly death nears your door! But I can promise you that death will not be the worst of it! Death will be just the beginning!"

The gypsy woman further manipulated her long, bony fingers into strange unnatural images, slow dances of bizarre description outlined obscene patterns and uncouth designs in the air before her—while the creature she now controlled—that she had caused to rise from the grave—moved as she willed it.

Now inside the house, the reanimated corpse of Amos LaRontue slowly trudged up the stairway and then down the hall to where the sounds of human lust were heard. Like a monster from hell the creature barreled *into* and *through* the bedroom door with a resounding explosion of splintered wood.

For a brief moment the dead thing stood framed in the doorway, the twilight moon from the skylight overhead giving the creature a ghastly aura. The pungent odor of death was atrocious.

Lamont LaRontue and Alice Carmody stared up at the ghastly thing frozen in a silent tableau of utter fear and shock, held in a fierce paroxysm of terror and apprehension as the thing—dripping bits of rotting flesh fresh with wriggling maggots—relentlessly ambled forward toward them.

"Amos? Is that you? My God!" Lamont shouted over the screams of the terrified girl beside him, for now he suddenly recognized the intruder as the reanimated corpse of his own dead brother. Though he could barely recognize the rotten rictus that smiled so hauntingly upon him, Lamont knew that this horrible thing from the grave could be none other than the remains of the brother he had murdered with his own hands scant months before.

"No, Amos! Don't do it! It was a mistake. I admit it, I wanted the girl. I wanted the house, the family fortune ... but this! You can't do this! We are still brothers and we will always be brothers!"

There was no reaction from the thing from the grave. It ignored the pleadings of the terrified man and the wild cries of the naked, shivering girl, but stood in silent contemplation as if awaiting orders.

Now Sabella's nimble fingers described a short arc in the hot summer air before her and Lamont saw the deteriorated features of his dead brother twist into a horrible grin of impending doom.

Lamont was so terrified by this vision, a vision that could only have come from the darkest depths of hell, that he could not move. He was so frozen in terror. In fact, he could not so much as scream his abject fear as the dead thing approached him, so fascinated was he by the appearance of the horrible image. He could not believe what he was seeing—almost—but his fear told him this was all only too real.

The dead thing drew closer and closer, its long, bony, white fingers worming their way around the man's neck, exerting a preternatural pressure. Hard and tight, those bloodless chilly fingers twisted, digging deep into the warm pink flesh, searing the delicate skin, choking off the life-giving flow of breath, and soon causing rivers of crimson to flow so freely down to the hungry floor boards below.

Finally, the dead creature's hunger asserted itself as it plunged its mouth into his own brother's neck, drinking the blood, feasting upon the flesh, rotted teeth cutting and tearing muscle and fat in ravenous bites as the dead thing feasted upon the warm human body it held prisoner. The devouring was a hellish thing to behold, the work of a demon with an insatiable appetite.

The girl, Alice Carmody, watching this abomination of horror and evil, screamed bloody murder and then fainted dead away. She was blessedly sparred the creature's beastly attention because of her condition.

Once the ghastly deed had been done, the thing from the grave carefully picked up the still warm corpus, the bloody remains of its own brother, and carried it in its outstretched arms out of the house, down the white-columned porch, and out into the clearing before LaRontue Mansion.

Here the creature stopped for a moment as ordered while Sabella took one last look and whispered a fond, "Farewell, Lamont! You spurned my love. Now you and your brother shall live in hell for eternity!"

Sabella laughed wildly, whipped a tear from her cheek and then gave the dead monster standing before her the last instructions that she thought it would ever receive this side of hell.

Sabella watched in rapt fascination as the dead thing carried the corpse of her dead lover—and its own brother—to shamble off into the stagnant heat of the dark Louisiana night. The thing moved off with deliberate design, down to the family plot near the walled garden in the back of the large house. Then it placed the body of Lamont, with unimagined and gentle consideration, into the soft earth of a newly excavated grave.

Finally the reanimated creature slowly lowered itself into that very same grave, using its long bony hands to cover itself with the dirt heaped in such high piles all around that grave.

Then the thing went back to sleep the eternal sleep of the dead, as the witch-woman had so ordered it to do until it was awakened once again.

Unless that grave was opened and the bodies disturbed.

Sabella, the witch-woman, now an ancient crone, cackled with insane delight at what she had wrought to pass through her devilish powers. Powers that had grown far beyond the realms of time and space itself to actually enable her to reanimate the very flesh and bones of the dead. That dark knowledge had disturbed her, and the use of it had taken a steep price from her, for she had never truly thought her revenge would work, nor be accomplished with such vile circumstance. The dark knowledge she'd had to access to perform such a rite had quite unhinged her mind, and changed her significantly, aging her greatly. Her once lovely beauty was now lost and replaced with a leathery visage that looked like it had newly come from the grave itself. The effect had destroyed her sanity. When she saw her visage in a reflection she screamed at the ghastly site. She was now hideous and her mad mind conjured up all kinds of new thoughts and schemes to take her revenge upon the people she blamed for her misfortune. Not one of them being herself, of course.

Slowly she shambled off into the heat of the dark Louisiana night with schemes of hatred and revenge as twisted plots and schemes against all living creatures burned into her mind.

Chapter 2: The Witness

**IRCH ELLROY**, THE SHERIFF of Macedonia Parish, had a headache that just wouldn't go away, no way, no how. He'd taken an Excedrin and then a Tylenol, but his head still hurt and his mind was speeding like a race horse that had just thrown its jockey.

"Alright, girl, take it easy now and tell me again what happened?" Ellroy asked softly, to the terrified village girl Alice Carmody.

Alice was sitting before the sheriff with her mother and father. The girl had been found wandering the road off the main highway, naked, shivering — even in the 100 degree humid Louisiana summer heat. She had seemingly lost all her senses, as well as all her clothing. She'd been rescued, taken to the hospital, then home, but she was unable to speak of what had happened to her for days. Her only verbal communication to her parents being wild screams about some "thing" she'd seen. Then she usually followed this by yelling bloody murder. She'd been taken to her parents' home in the village and after a few days the doctor said she was well enough to answer a few questions. That's when Sheriff Ellroy had been called in to have a few minutes with her, but it wasn't easy.

The sheriff hardly knew what to make of the girl's strange story. It had been a monumental task to get her to even speak at all — much less coherently — about what she said she had witnessed that night some days ago.

Just what had she seen?

Ellroy thought about that as he waited for the girl to collect her thoughts and repeat her story. A murder? At least it appeared that's what she was saying. But something else too, something not quite right at all seemed to be going on at LaRontue Mansion.

That was bad. The place had a reputation in the parish and the people who had lived there throughout the years always had been trouble. The old man had been bad enough, but Ellroy figured his two sons, Amos and Lamont, might be even worse. Then when Amos went missing about two months ago... Well, things never did seem right with that situation. Lamont, when asked, said his brother had gone away, to visit relatives up in New York City, but that just didn't sit right with Ellroy. Why the heck would Amos go off to a place like New York City all of a sudden? But without any evidence, with not even a missing persons report, he had little to go on. The man was an adult after all, so he could go where he wanted, whenever he wanted, and if he wanted to go out on his own it was his right. There was no indication of foul play. It just seemed so unlike him to leave his family home. He was a LaRontue, they had all been born there and they had all died there from before the Revolution, almost two hundred years ago.

Some people said the old house was haunted of course, from way back since that time during the Civil War when something dark and evil happened there to some Union troops. But since it was "blue-bellies" that had the problem not many of the old time Southerners cared much back then. Still and all, the rumors had been disturbing.

Others just said it was that crazy gypsy witch-woman, Sabella, who caused all the rumors. It was known Lamont had a thing for Sabella; her exotic, dark beauty, her mysterious witchy ways. She could sure tempt a man, Ellroy mused. But he'd never been interested in her. He had to admit that he was just a little scared of her. Anyway, he hadn't seen her in a long time either. She seemed to have run off too now. She was nowhere to be found.

Now this situation with Alice had been thrown in his lap.

"Come on, Alice," Ellroy prompted, growing impatient. "Tell me what happened out there?" He wanted to get something from her today, now and on paper, so as not to have to come back tomorrow, or day after day, until she spoke up about what had happened.

The girl nodded with dogged determination to repeat her strange tale once again, but the fear in her eyes made it a most delicate matter, for all could see she was battling powerful unseen inner demons. She was terrified. Shaking with abject fear.

"Just tell Sheriff Ellroy the truth, darling, just what you saw, Alice," her mother prompted softly, brushing back the long golden tresses from her daughter's young but tense face.

Those eyes, Ellroy though, they were dead things starring off into space, unfocused, as if they were light bulbs blown out by a sudden surge of electricity. The girl had seen something all right, Ellroy was certain. It had right properly blown her mind. Ellroy just hoped this version of the story would give him something to go on. He hadn't been out to LaRontue Mansion in many years, but he knew that would have to change soon. He was not looking forward to it.

Alice Carmody looked around her sharply, as if what she feared so much might be in the very house with her, right in that very room!

Or maybe even right behind her!

"I saw it!" she cried, rocking her body back and forth, still in traumatic shock. "It came for him. It was alive! Alive! How can that be? I recognized him, you see. It was him—the brother..."

"Amos?" Sheriff Ellroy blurted.

Alice Carmody ignored the question as she continued to stare off into the wall at the opposite end of the room. It was a light blue-colored wall with a hanging painting depicting a lovely pastoral Louisiana landscape. But that's not what the girl was seeing there at all now. She was looking beyond what was there—deep into somewhere else... far away...

"Maggots! They were on it—everywhere!" she screamed, then shuddered, remembering. Her mother hugged her closely looking at the sheriff, her eyes begging him to stop the questions for now.

"Can't you see she's not well, Sheriff," Nancy Carmody pleaded. The girl's father nodded in sad agreement, for it was clear to all that Alice's mind had snapped, severely damaged by something terrible she had seen that fateful night.

Ellroy nodded reluctantly, he knew he had no choice but to back off for now.

"Lamont's dead!" the girl suddenly barked, growled madly. "*It* killed him!" Then the girl screamed and passed out.

Ellroy shook his head, he'd get no more from her today. She was shot. He felt bad for the girl, and the parents. "I'm sorry for what happened and hope your daughter recovers soon, Mr. and Mrs. Carmody. I'll check out what she's told me so far."

"Best to see what them people are up to out there," Ben Carmody said sharply. "What did they do to her? My poor, poor, Alice!"

"Up to no good is what they're up to!" Nancy Carmody blurted out with harsh bitterness as she hugged her daughter tightly, tears streaming from her eyes now. "It's them boys, Amos and Lamont. Bad seeds, I tell you! They was always after our sweet lovely Alice. Now something terrible has happened...

Sheriff Birch Ellroy nodded, "I'll get to the bottom of this."

"Best get your ass out to LaRontue Mansion then," the mother scolded, rocking her daughter tightly in her arms.

Ellroy allowed a grim smile to come to his face at the no nonsense talk from this no nonsense woman. "I was just fixin' to go out there, ma'am."

Chapter 3: The Investigation

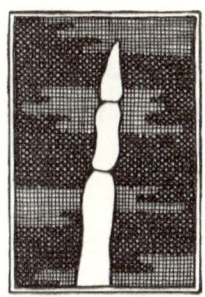

T WAS A LONG DRIVE out to the ancestral home of the LaRontue Family. They'd been big once in Louisiana politics. Huey Long himself had even used the house as his governor's mansion the year he'd been assassinated. Bad luck seemed to follow the place. Then there were tales of ghosts and haunting as far back as when the French and Spanish had held sway over Louisiana, when it had been the Louisiana Territory long before it had ever been a part of the United States. Indians told other stories about the area, much darker. They stayed away, even today.

Sheriff Birch Ellroy shook his head, determined not to allow old superstitions and rumors sway him from doing his job. He prided himself on being a common sense man and always being logical. For him there was no other way for a man to be, especially an officer of the law. Nevertheless, something had happened out here a few nights ago and he was going to get to the bottom of it.

His temples throbbed with pain as he drove the long highway out into the bayou, a lonely rural part of Macedonia Parish. This was wild country, Cajun and Indian territory, backwoods dangerous if you didn't know your druthers and didn't now your place with the people who lived out here. They were a lone and private, righteous independent bunch. They were the salt of the earth, and would go out of their way to help you for any reason, but if you ever crossed them or did them dirty, they could just as easily plant you into that earth.

It took Elroy the better part of an hour to get out to the house. The sun was up and the warmth of the day was just beginning to settle in. His headache seemed to be winding down and he hoped he would get in and out quick on this job—find out what happened, fix it, and then get it over with fast.

At least, he could dream.

After all, maybe this would prove to be only the wild fancies of a young girl. Maybe with some rougher than usual sex, some drugs or booze mixed in, the usual kind of thing. Maybe it was some wild story made up by the girl to get her parents off her back for her escapades? It wouldn't be the first time a girl had made up a story to save herself from parental punishment, Ellroy knew, but Alice's story and the look in her eyes seemed to belie any of that. Alice was either the best little damn actress in the world, or something along the lines of what she'd said had actually happened. That was certainly disturbing, whatever it might actually be. She'd been found on the highway stark naked and in what could only have been shock or a drug-induced state so . . .

Even as he thought about it Ellroy felt there had to be something more to all this, something dark and potentially much more deadly. He knew he had to check it out more deeply.

Sheriff Birch Ellroy drove up to the large black wrought iron gate and found it unlocked and open. He got out of his Jeep and hit the buzzer on the box attached to the wall to announce to the house his presence on the property.

There was no reply. He shrugged, so much the better. He got back into his Jeep and drove down the tree-lined road towards the big house. Two minutes later he was driving up the gravel oval driveway, parked his Jeep and walked over to the front door of LaRontue Mansion.

Ellroy stopped dead in his tracks as he took his first good look at the stately old house in many years. He'd not been out this way since he had been a teenager taking out girls, and drinking beer with his friends. Drinking and necking in the surrounding bayou, he'd seen the old house lurking in the background like it was watching them. However they'd always stayed away from that house. Old Man LaRontue was the main reason he'd been alive back then and he was a nasty, mean bugger, with a good aim on that shotgun of his. Ellroy and his friends never went too near the house and they never hung with young Amos and Lamont. The boy who would eventually grow to manhood to become the parish sheriff and the two LaRontue Brothers were from different worlds entirely.

Ellroy looked up at the house and stared at it for a good ten minutes as if transfixed. The place exuded menace. It looked the same as it always had, as if time had somehow stopped here. It was a large antebellum plantation mansion, in the Southern French style, red tile roof, a lot of intricate black wrought iron railings on the first floor and around the second floor windows. The place was dark, no lights, windows covered by heavy curtains. Everything about the place made it seem dreary and cold. Ellroy felt a chill creep up his spine.

They—*they* being some of the locals—said the place was haunted. Ellroy had heard all the rumors of course, but always discarded them. That was all nonsense he would never allow himself to consider. He was a logical man, after all, and proud of the fact. Even when he thought of Amos and Lamont's father, Old Man LaRontue. Now what was his name? Mark David LaRontue. They had called him Mad Mark. The old man had hung himself years ago from the chandelier in the inside foyer of his very own house. He'd been discovered by a maid, who had instantly had a heart attack from the stress of her discovery. She had keeled over and died the same day. It was real bad mojo all around and the news got the whole village talking for months.

Ellroy shook his head as if trying to break a spell, but he couldn't look away from that dark and malignant building. He also wondered why no one had come out of the house to meet him by now. It was most unusual for anyone, even the sheriff, to drive onto the grounds of these old mansions without someone confronting him. Even if the owners were away, there should be a groundskeeper or some household staff working in the place. The gates were never left opened either. It was unusual, but perhaps there was a logical explanation for it all?

Ellroy sighed deeply, rubbed his throbbing head as he walked up to the ornate mahogany front door of the place and rang the bell.

The sheriff intended to speak to Lamont LaRontue about the girl, see what he could find out. He waited, expecting any moment for a maid or butler to answer his ring but no one came to the door.

He rang again and again but there was no response.

Sheriff Birch Ellroy drew his .45 and then reached out towards the handle of the front door of LaRontue Mansion. It was unlocked. Now his alarm bells really went up a notch. He considered calling for backup but he knew his only deputy, Herman Sikes, was off working on a case all the way at the other end of the parish. It would take Herman a good hour or more to get out here. Better for him to just go inside now and see what he could see. So that's what he did.

"Hello! Anyone here?"

There was no response.

No sound at all answered his call.

Ellroy checked his weapon to ensure it was ready to be used. It was. He hoped this would not be the time he used it.

The sheriff called out again, this time much louder and still there was no response.

Damn, that was weird, he thought. These big houses usually had a staff of maids, or at least a butler and a cook. It seemed like there was no one here at all.

"Lamont LaRontue, I'm Sheriff Ellroy and I need to talk to you," he shouted, then repeated his words even louder.

His pleas were met without any response.

He felt that cold shiver down his back again and he didn't like it at all — but his headache had definitely gone away by now. He didn't know which feeling he hated more.

Ellroy carefully walked into the house, gun drawn, leaving the door open behind him. He looked with care at the luxurious furniture, valuable paintings, all the trappings of wealth and power that were evident throughout the entrance hall and up the long winding stairway. He noted these, but also noted their worn and old appearance, as if neglect and the passage of time had its dire effect upon the things inside the house, just as it had upon the house itself. He grew careful, not knowing what to expect. He held his weapon ready and then began a systematic room by room search of the downstairs part of the mansion.

He found no one on the entire first floor and when he called out once again, no one replied.

"This is growing spookier by the minute," he heard himself say.

Then he took a deep breath and began a slow and careful walk up the winding, creaky old staircase to check out the rooms on the second floor.

Once in the upstairs landing he noticed there were eight bedrooms, four on each side of the floor that opened out onto the landing, each with their own bathroom.

"Nice to be rich," he muttered softly.

Dead silence answered him.

He began to search the second floor, room by room, methodically and by the book, with alert caution. Six of the rooms seemed to be generic, probably spare bedrooms for overnight guests. They were empty. The next one was obviously the bedroom of the missing brother, Amos, or so evidence indicated. Again, it told him nothing. The remaining bedroom obviously belonged to the other brother, Lamont. It was there that Ellroy found the signs of a struggle and saw a brown patch of what might be dried blood upon the carpet.

"Maybe you saw a murder after all, girl," Ellroy muttered to himself. Then he used his cell phone to call it in.

Chapter 4: Missing Men

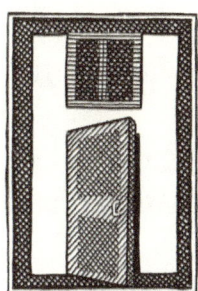**OURS** LATER ELLROY'S DEPUTY, Herman Sikes, arrived with the parish Medical Examiner, Doctor Howard Carter. Carter took photos and samples off the carpet, while Sikes dusted the room and the rest of the house for prints. Ellroy watched the two men working and tried to imagine what the hell had happened here. Had there been a murder? And where was Lamont LaRontue? Had he murdered his brother and then skipped? There was no one in the house to ask, no family, no staff, no one.

Ellroy decided to run a state-wide missing persons BOLO on Lamont, see what came up. He also ran a BOLO on the missing brother, Amos. Then he called Trudy at the *Macedonia Post*, the local newspaper, to see if she could find any next of kin or family for Lamont. Maybe they would know something?

It was Doc Carter who got his attention. "I'm just about to finish up here, Birch. I'd bet the stain is blood. I've got some luminal back in the truck but I think we can safely say that without using it. I'll check it out anyway, of course. Whether or not it's Lamont's blood or not, we'll have to wait for that result."

"Yeah, that's fine, Howie."

"One thing," Carter said with a tired look in his eyes,

"I found these at various places in the room here. On the carpet, and out in the hall and on the steps."

Carter opened his hand, and showed them to the sheriff. They looked like pieces of rice at first.

"They're dead now, of course."

"What are they?"

"Maggots."

"What the hell? What would they be doing here in the bedroom?"

"Don't know. They live off a dead host, eat it, then turn into flies. These fell off something, they starved and died," Carter said matter-of-factly.

"What does that mean?" Ellroy asked the doctor.

"Damned if I know," Carter shrugged with a laugh. He put the maggot carcasses into a clear plastic baggie and closed it, labeled it, then started to collect his things.

"What do you think happened here, Howie?"

The M.E. shook his head. "We don't get many murders in this parish, Birch. Haven't seen one for years. Especially among the rich and powerful, but I'd say you've got yourself a doozie now."

"Yeah, thanks."

Carter laughed good-naturedly, "I'll let you know when the DNA comes back, see if that blood belongs to Lamont LaRontue."

"Okay, thanks," Ellroy said as Carter packed up and left. Then he gave his attention to his deputy. "Herman? What you got?"

Ellroy's deputy, Herman Sikes, came into the room from where he'd been dusting for prints in the outer hallway.

"I did the room, the hall and the stairway rail. Got a lot of prints. It will take some time to match them with what we have on file to see if we can pick up anyone not supposed to be in the house."

"Yeah, sounds like a long shot to me."

"It is. I took over a hundred prints, my bet is they'll all prove to be family members, servants, guests, friends, no killer."

"Yeah, if there was a killer, *he* probably wore gloves."

"Or it is an outside agency, that we have nothing on in our files, like some vagrant."

"Nice," Ellroy said; he had been thinking the same thing and his headache was beginning to come back with a vengeance now. That could really complicate things. It was getting dark and he wanted to wrap it up for the day. "I want you to run these prints down anyway and let me know if you find anything. I'll be back here first light tomorrow to do a check on the grounds."

"You got a hunch, boss? You want me to call in some help?" Sikes asked curiously. He was excited that they apparently had a real major crime on their hands here. He'd never been involved in the likes before. It made him feel important, part of something big and maybe newsworthy.

"Not yet, I just want to look around in the daylight, see what I can see."

Chapter 5: The Story Grows

 **HAT** NIGHT BIRCH ELLROY told his wife the entire strange story at dinner. Susie Ellroy was surprised and upset by what had happened to Alice Carmody, who she knew somewhat from the village. It was hard to hear about the girl being found naked out on the highway in the middle of nowhere. She only hoped Macedonia wasn't becoming like the big cities they'd left behind them, when they'd come out here to small town Louisiana. Then there was that rumor about Amos LaRontue having gone off somewhere unknown, and now his brother, Lamont, had apparently gone missing.

"Think she killed him, Birch?" Susie said casually as they ate dinner. Twelve year old Thomas, who liked to be called Tommy, listened in rapt attention but he knew better than to speak up when his Ma and Pa were talking police business. Tommy and his Ma also knew that the words spoken around the table regarding police business were never meant to be spoken about to anyone else in Macedonia Parish—and they never were.

"I don't know. The girl's a mess—confused, terrified. She saw something out there. It doesn't seem like any act to me, but you can never be certain. Not yet. What happened? I really don't know."

"Maybe she saw Bigfoot?" Tommy offered, trying to

be helpful. He was referring to some legends about that part of the bayou he had seen on a Monsterquest TV show on the History Channel the night before.

Birch Ellroy just laughed with good-natured warmth. "I don't think so, Tommy, but I appreciate your advice."

Tommy smiled.

"Finish up your dinner now," Sue Ellroy told her son. "Then you can go to your room and play X-box for one hour before you go to sleep, okay?"

"Cool, mom!" Tommy chowed down the last of his food, cleaning his plate, and was gone in a flash leaving his ma and pa alone in the small dining room.

"That boy has some imagination," Birch laughed.

"He gets it from you."

"Oh, no, don't put that on me. He gets it from you. You're the one with the imagination, you're the book writer in the family."

"I write Harlequin romances, Birch, it's hardly the same thing," Sue replied, picking up the plates and bringing them into the kitchen and placing them into the sink. Birch helped her.

"So, what was it like out there?"

"I can't explain it…"

"I mean the house."

"Spooky. I don't know. I was out of sorts all day, had a bad headache, a migraine I guess, so I can't say for sure, but I kept having this strange feeling…"

She came over to him, rubbed herself up against him and then put her arms around his neck pulling him closer to her.

He smiled, "Not *that* kind of feeling, Sue."

"I know, honey. But you seem so tense."

"I am."

"So, what type of feeling then?" she asked curious.

"It was unnerving, it made me anxious. I felt a coldness out there that didn't seem … well, it didn't seem natural. The day was hot and humid and yet I felt a weird chill that went right in my bones—it was stronger in the upstairs bedroom."

"Where you found the bloody carpet?"

"Yeah, right there. Even Howie and Herman remarked upon it later when we talked things over."

"That is strange."

"Yeah."

"So, where's Lamont LaRontue?"

Birch Ellroy shrugged, "Your guess is as good as mine. The missing persons report showed nothing. I asked Trudy at the *Post* to put me in contact with other members of the family, to see if maybe they had heard something …"

"And?"

"Well, they're a weird bunch, let me tell you. There's some cousins and aunts over at Biloxi, but they won't have anything to do with this branch of the family."

"Really."

"They told me they won't involve themselves with 'those people' as they called them."

"Well that's weird, and it's not very nice," she replied.

"Yeah, well they don't seem like a very nice bunch, Sue."

They were silent for a few minutes. Then they moved over to the couch in the living room, sat down together, holding each other.

"What's your next move?" she asked.

"You're very inquisitive this evening, Mrs. Ellroy?" Birch said as he playfully grabbed her to him and kissed her long and hard.

"Police business first, sheriff, then monkey business, if you please," Sue said, squirming out of his embrace.

Birch shook his head in mock annoyance.

Sue waited.

"Howie's doing a DNA on the blood, but I don't expect any results for some days. I've got Herman checking the database for prints. It will take him all day tomorrow, maybe longer. I doubt he'll turn up anything good, but ..."

"And what about you? You going to talk to that girl again?"

"Not yet. I want to give her more time to get herself... I don't know, Sue, she troubles me. She's about as close to being insane as anyone I've ever seen," Birch said.

"Maybe she was always a bit ... you know, like that to begin with? Some of these younger gals can be awfully dramatic," she offered.

"I know, but I don't think that's true with her. She saw something that really freaked her out. She can't even talk about it in any coherent way."

"Really, she's that bad?"

"Yeah, you should have seen her. And she ... You know, she mentioned maggots too!" Birch said thoughtfully now.

"Maggots? Eeek!"

"No, I mean, she mentioned maggots on the thing that scared her and then Howie—Doctor Carter—he showed me something he found in the house today. Dead maggots."

Sue didn't say anything about that; she didn't know what to say.

"Weird, eh?" Birch asked.

"So what are you going to do?"

"First thing tomorrow, I'm going back there, check out things thoroughly; the house, the grounds. I have a feeling I'm missing something and that there's a lot more to this than there seems to be."

"Well, good luck, I haven't been out that way since … uh …"

"I know, since you and I and Frankie and Kathleen and the Rogers sisters and the Amboy twins went out that way drinking and necking — like 15 years ago."

She hit him gently with a tight little fist, lovingly, "Oh, you! It wasn't 15 years!"

"Yes it was," he insisted, amazed himself at the passage of time. So many years had gone by so fast he had almost lost count. They'd been so young, once.

She thought about it, sighed. "You're right, Birch, I guess it was. Damn!"

"Anyway, that's what's on the agenda for tomorrow. What's on the agenda for tonight?"

She got up from the couch and coyly walked away from him, "Well, if the sheriff takes a walk into the bedroom in about five minutes, he will surely find out."

Chapter 6: The Grave

**EXT** MORNING, Sheriff Birch Ellroy once again took the long drive out along the highway to the end of Macedonia Parish where LaRontue Mansion stood in lonely macabre seclusion. In the morning light it was a lovely drive through brush and bayou and he had a lot to think about on the way out there. His headache had come back and he popped a couple of Tylenol, hoping they'd work and spare him the pain. He didn't expect much relief.

It was a long and lonely drive and the closer he came to LaRontue Mansion, the more that eerie feeling seemed to creep up on him again. It wasn't so much the cold this time as the prickling of the hairs on the back of his neck.

Birch Ellroy thought of himself as a good sheriff. He'd been a New Orleans cop for years before Katrina. After that mess he'd moved back here to Macedonia because he and Sue thought things would be better. It was a small, close-knit community and he knew most of the people from when he'd been a kid. He became the sheriff and Sue wrote her books. And they both had Tommy. So they'd been happy, and everything had been right in their world. Until now. Now he knew something wasn't right, and he had a bad feeling about it.

Ellroy had been a cop for 12 years and all his senses and hunches told him today that he was on the edge of something he may have never encountered before and it scared him. It scared him and he couldn't shake the feeling of strangeness—and even evil—he felt around it all.

When the sheriff reached the LaRontue estate he saw the front gates were opened. That was odd because he'd closed them last evening after he'd left and put up yellow crime scene tape. Now the gate was open and the tape was gone. He drove on through, down the tree-lined lane towards the circular driveway.

A car was parked there, a small red Toyota. He knew that car and sighed with exasperation. It was the press, and he got that feeling cops get whenever the press were on a case, nosing around, taking photos, asking all kinds of questions. Then he reminded himself that he wasn't in New Orleans any longer, but in Macedonia Parish, and this was just Trudy Nelson; publisher, editor, reporter and photog for the local *Macedonian Post*. And even though she was what passed for the local press, she was also a friend. She was also nowhere in sight.

He met her coming out of the house, as he was walking in.

"Hey, Birch, how's things?" the power behind the local press—such as it was—asked with a perky brightness. Trudy Nelson was a thirty-something divorcee from the big city with one kid and two cats. She was all right.

"Hey, Trudy," Ellroy replied none too happy she'd been inside the house without him or Herman being present. It was also obvious she'd been taking photos. The place was still a crime scene but he didn't see any tape across the front door. Herman either forgot to place it there last night, or she had taken it off.

"You know you're not supposed to—"

She cut him off, "Come on, Birch, we're all family here. You or Herman forgot the tape so I went in and took a look. No harm done."

"What about the tape I put up at the outer gate, which I had closed on my way out last night?" he stated, looking at her sharply.

"Oh, Birch, well..."

"Trudy."

"Come on, Birch," she pleaded softly. "I helped you with the relatives, didn't I? By the way, what panned out with them?"

"Nothing," he stated.

"Nothing. Now that's a bit vague. Come on."

"All right, but don't say you got it from me, understand?"

"Sure, Birch, I know the rules."

"The relatives don't know anything about anything that happened here or the whereabouts of Lamont. In fact, they told me they don't have anything to do with this side of the family—'those people'—as they called them, at all."

"Really?"

"Yeah, really."

"Cold bunch?"

"You could say that. The entire family seems that way."

"So what do you think?" she asked allowing her natural curiosity to show.

"I don't know yet. By the way, did you take any photos inside?"

"Just a few," she said demurely.

Ellroy sighed. "Wait a day or two and ask me before you run them, okay?"

"Okay, Birch."

They looked at each other. He liked Trudy, but she was still the press. Even though she ran a small local paper, practically a penny-saver with delusions of grandeur, she was still the press. Hence, for any cop, the enemy.

"I want to talk to that girl, Birch," Trudy asked a bit more forcefully, "but the parents keep putting me off."

"She's in bad shape, give her a week or so," Ellroy told her.

Trudy digested that. She did not intend to wait that long. Instead she asked, "You ran an APB, anything come up on Lamont?"

"No."

"That's interesting. You think she killed him?" Trudy was referring to the girl, Alice, having murdered Lamont.

"Now, Trudy," Ellroy replied, taking her by the arm and escorting her away from the front door, "don't you go spreading rumors or jumping to conclusions. So far, the girl's clean, she's been through enough, so don't go making life more difficult for her—and me—by printing anything that's not solid. You hear me?"

"So then you believe her story." It was a statement, not a question.

"Yes, some of it, maybe most of it. Aw, hell, I don't know for sure yet, but she sure as hell saw something weird that night—now don't you be putting any of that in your paper, either!"

"All right, Birch, I'll hold off for the time being but you'll let me know what happens when you know?"

Ellroy sighed, his headache was growing, he needed to keep his temper in check. "Sure."

They walked on a bit, silent, both thinking their own thoughts.

"So what are you doing out here on this fine summer morning?" she asked.

He smiled, he didn't want to answer and she knew it.

"Come on," she prodded.

"Just looking around," he answered reluctantly.

"Mind if I tag along?"

Ellroy looked at the woman, but kept his temper in check. The last thing he wanted or needed was to have Trudy Nelson and her camera up his ass and interfering with him while he was out here looking around. But he couldn't very well order her off—or if he did—that would be worse. She'd glom onto that right away and know something was up for sure. Then she would become an actual problem rather than just a mere annoyance to his work. The sheriff sighed resignedly, forced a smile, "Free country."

"That's great, Birch. You know, I think this could be the beginning of a beautiful friendship," she said with a flippant voice and a slight wink.

Birch Ellroy growled silently to himself, annoyed by her words because she'd paraphrased a section from the end of one of his favorite films, *Casablanca*. He was not Bogart and she was certainly not Claude Rains. This was not going to become any partnership.

Ellroy tried a different tack, said confidentially, "It's going to be a long, boring day out here in the hot sun, Trudy. Sure you don't want to get back to your nice air-conditioned office and work on your newspaper? I can call you if anything important is discovered."

"Nah, I have Joey Ross there as a part-time intern, he's helping out and doing a good job," she replied giving him a wry grin. She knew he was trying to dissuade her from staying here with him but it wasn't going to work—and the sheriff knew it as well now. "I'm free as long as I need to be, Birch. Nothing for me to do all day but hang with you. Aren't you lucky!"

Ellroy growled more verbally this time, shook his head, "Well, then just … Please, stay out of the way."

Birch Ellroy had to admit that Trudy Nelson was a good egg. Even if she was doing her own modern version of Brenda Starr, Girl Reporter. She stayed out of his way, she didn't ask a lot of annoying questions, and she didn't take any photographs of him as he investigated the grounds around the mansion. Well, maybe just one photo, when she thought he wasn't looking. He let that one slide.

She did ask him what he was looking for and he'd replied that he didn't know just yet, which was actually the truth.

She followed him like a lost puppy as he trod around the grounds, at first flush up against the huge house, moving around and away from it slowly, in a careful search pattern. Then he walked an outward arc that took them farther and farther from the house. That's when Ellroy noticed the patch of dirt.

"That looks like a grave, Birch," Trudy blurted with excitement as they walked closer. She quickly got off a photo.

"Trudy!" Birch growled in alarm. "I said no photos!"

"It's good documentation — for you, Birch," she told him. He didn't believe her for a minute, but …

"Okay, so long as you understand that from this point on you're not here in the capacity of the press.

You are now a duly authorized police photographer for Macedonia Parish — and as such you are here under my direct orders. You understand that?" he asked sharply, before he allowed her to move one more step.

"Yes, I understand the rules, Birch, we've done this before, you know."

"I know, I just want you to be sure *you* know the rules, Trudy."

"Okay! Okay! Let's get on with it."

"I'll release the photos for you to publish when I can do so."

"Yes, all right, Birch. Now can we see what we have here."

"What we have here is a freshly dug grave," Ellroy told her.

"Yes!" Trudy shouted in excitement as she began taking more photos from all different angles.

Ellroy sighed, may as well let her do her job. He looked at the grave more closely now. It was fresh. Well, then, here it was. Now the case would really begin. He took out his cell phone and began the calls. "Don't touch anything. I'm calling Herman and Howie to have them get back out here. We'll have to dig up this grave — if it is a grave — and see what we have. If anything."

"Oh, it's a grave, Birch, don't you fret on that score," Trudy said confidently.

Yes, he had to admit she was right, and that was what he was afraid of.

Chapter 7: Two Bodies

 **HEY** WAITED TWO HOURS in the hot Louisiana sun before Deputy Herman Sikes and the Parish M.E., Doctor Howard Carter arrived. Ellroy had not wanted to mess up any potential evidence without the doc being there before they began the excavation.

"Hey, Birch, I hear you found something," Sikes asked as he and the doc, still with Trudy Nelson present, made their way to the patch of ground behind the house near the woods.

"This is kinda becoming a regular thing out here," Doctor Carter said with a hint of concern in his voice. "So I hear you found a grave?"

"I think so," Ellroy replied as he led the way towards it.

"Well, one way to find out," Carter replied.

"That's why I called you and Herman."

"So let's get to it," Sikes said all fueled up and ready. He'd brought shovels and a pick from the trunk of his patrol car and began giving them out to the two men.

"Easy with those, boys," Carter advised. "You won't need the pick, the soil is soft from the recent rain. Use them shovels gingerly, we don't want to damage any evidence."

Ellroy nodded, took a shovel. "Like this, just pick up a little bit of dirt at the tip of the shovel, a little bit at a time. I don't think there's any coffin down here, so you'll not hit any wood, only what's left of someone's body. So be careful."

Deputy Sikes nodded, and the two men got to work. Doctor Carter watched and Trudy Nelson took more photos. She was as excited as she'd ever been since she'd moved into Macedonia from New Jersey and bought the *Post*. This could be the biggest story in the state, a famous murder case of all things, and she was right dab smack in the middle of it straight from the get-go!

Ellroy and Sikes dug gingerly, carefully, slowly, so as not to damage or disturb any evidence that might be in the grave. They didn't dig too deep before Sikes came up with something. His last shovel of dirt showed a bit of rotted clothing and when he brushed it away, there was dark, rotted flesh. It was an arm. And maggots. Lots of maggots.

Trudy Nelson watched in horror and disgust; she'd stopped taking photos.

It was a dead body.

Doctor Carter moved closer to the grave, took out a small garden shovel, and what looked like a large paint bush and began to carefully clean the dirt away from the body.

"It's a man, all right," Carter said as he got more involved in his work. Ellroy and Sikes helped as best they could and soon they had cleared away a lot of the dirt and opened the grave up.

"Birch," Carter said with evident surprise, "you got two bodies in this here grave."

"Two?"

"Yeah, definitely two. See how they're wrapped around each other? It will take some doing to separate them properly. I'll have to do that back at the morgue. Best you call Hank Youley now and have him bring out his hearse to transport the bodies."

At the Macedonian Parish morgue, Hank Youely, the local funeral home owner, dropped off the two bodies discovered in the unmarked grave behind LaRontue Mansion. The sheriff and his deputy took the entwined bodies out of the hearse and placed them onto Doctor Carter's autopsy table. Carter got set to do his work while Ellroy, Sikes and Trudy Nelson stood off at the side and watched with a mixture of wonder and disgust.

"One of these men is surely Lamont LaRontue," Herman Sikes stated confidently. "I know him by sight. Not much left of him now of course, but I'd say he's been dead less than two weeks."

"Could be," Carter admitted. "We'll know more once I'm done here."

"Then who's the other man?" Trudy Nelson asked. She didn't take any photos here, knowing the Doc would never allow such a thing.

"Don't know yet," Carter said as he continued his work, "but this other body's been dead somewhat longer, a couple months longer."

"Could it be Amos LaRontue?" Ellroy asked allowing his suspicions full vent. Now he felt a shiver, and a dark thought nagged at his mind—had the girl, Alice, killed both of these men?

Sikes and Trudy, even Carter, looked at the sheriff, but none of them said a word.

Sheriff Birch Ellroy looked at the entwined bodies of the two dead men upon the autopsy table and he got that cold feeling running up and down his back again. Like spiders crawling all over him.

"It's cold in here," Trudy Nelson observed, suddenly shivering. "Isn't it cold in here?"

"I have the air on," Carter explained, "an autopsy room's supposed to be cool."

Trudy shivered, nodded, then looked down at the bodies and shivered again, "That's so weird, the two of them wrapped together like that."

"Sure seems strange to me," Sikes added, watching the doctor do his work, not liking to watch but unable to look away.

"You having trouble, doc?" Ellroy had noticed a change in the man's mood.

"I don't know, Birch," Carter said softly. He'd been trying to separate the two bodies but they were so powerfully entwined, so tightly locked together in some weird kind of death embrace, that it seemed almost impossible to separate them. "Damned if I know. They're locked together worse than two peas in a pod. I'll clean them off, take some tissue samples, and then Trudy can take her photos for the file."

"Sure, Howie," Ellroy said.

"Look, boys, it's getting kinda late and Mrs. Carter don't like me out 'til all hours of the evening, like when we was young. I'll do what I can now, then refrigerate them and I'll finish this up tomorrow morning, separate them then. Okay?"

"Sure," Ellroy said, a bit disappointed, "You're the doctor."

"And don't you ever forget it!" Carter said with a hearty laugh. "You guys can leave now, nothing more left to do here. I have to finish up some of this paper work then I'm going on home."

With that said, Sheriff Ellroy left the morgue and went back to his own office with Deputy Sikes to finish up some police reports.

Trudy Nelson went on back to her paper to write up tomorrow's amazing news story and Doctor Howard Carter, tired and taking a well-deserved break left the two bodies on his table while he stepped outside to have a much needed cigarette. It had been a long day.

Chapter 8: No Bodies

**OCTOR** CARTER NEVER GOT A CHANCE to have that cigarette he had been wanting and needing so much. Doris, his wife, didn't like him to smoke, and as a doctor and at his age, he knew the health risks only too well, but he still liked a smoke now and then. So he did cheat sometimes. Long as Doris didn't know, he figured it was all right. However, that night, just as he'd stepped out of his medical office building located in the center of the village, he'd met Jake Burlingame and the two had struck up a talk that seemed to go on and on about what had happened out at LaRontue Mansion.

By the time Carter remembered why he'd come outside in the first place—to take a cigarette break from the autopsy—he realized he still had two cold stiffs laying on the slab inside. He felt a bit guilty at wasting so much time and of leaving the bodies out for so long—not that he thought the two dead guys would mind—but he liked to think of himself as a professional and he liked to do his work in a professional way. He also had to get on home to Doris before she worried and started to make phone calls.

When Carter went back inside the building and saw what awaited him upon the autopsy table he just stared with shock and utter disbelief.

"Where the hell are they?" Carter muttered softly, scratching his head.

The two dead bodies were gone!

Doctor Howard Carter could hardly believe it.

"What the hell!" he shouted now, losing his patience. "This better not be some damn prank!"

Carter looked all over the small building for the missing bodies but they were nowhere to be found. He didn't want to allow any crazy thoughts about them getting up and walking away but he had a weird feeling about this; he couldn't help having dark thoughts pop into his head. He stopped them from forming right away. Such thoughts were ridiculous. Thinking in that direction was utter nonsense; after all he was a doctor, a scientist, by God!

"Be logical, dammit!" he growled, looking around the empty room as if the two bodies would suddenly reappear and then everything would be back to normal. They didn't. This wasn't normal at all. Where the hell were they?

Man, did he need that cigarette now!

Carter calmed himself and walked back to the table and looked at it and the area surrounding it more closely. He noted the lingering death smell, which was atrocious now, and seemingly fresh. The bodies had been foul before, but the odor had been nothing like it was now—and the bodies weren't even here. Then he noticed the stuff that was left, tiny pieces of rotted clothing and flesh, dissolving skin and tissue, maggots—maggots everywhere—like they had fallen off the bodies.

Carter shook his head in exasperation. He didn't like this kind of thing. Someone had obviously come in here and carried off his damn bodies. It had to be a prank.

A pretty sick prank at that! That was the only possible explanation. Carter thought of those kids at the high school, some of those boys could get pretty wild at times...

He rang up the sheriff and was glad to find him in.

"What's up, Howie?" Ellroy asked, surprised to hear from the doctor so late. "How you doing on that autopsy? I thought you'd be home by now having a late dinner with Doris. Everything okay?"

"Yeah, ah... well, Birch, that's what I'm calling about. Look, I don't know how to say this so I'll just say it."

"Sure."

"I went outside for a cigarette, and I met Jake Burlingame..."

"How's old Jake?"

"Yeah, he's fine, but listen, we got to talking and I let go of the time. When I got back inside and went over to work on the bodies—they were gone."

"Gone?"

"That's what I said. No joke, Birch, they're gone and I can't find 'em."

Ellroy was quiet for a moment. Was this some kind of a joke? Carter playing games with him? Nah, that wasn't like Howie at all. Then Ellroy got that creepy feeling running up and down his back again. He also felt the mother of all headaches coming on, very sudden like.

Sheriff Ellroy took a deep breath. "Howie, you sure about this? This better not be some kind of joke, I got no patience for that sort of thing right now."

"Come on, Birch, I'm not kidding. They're gone. I looked all over. Maybe those kids at the high school did it, you know? They're always playing pranks or doing some mischief. That's all I can figure."

"Nah, I really don't think it's that, but I guess it has to be ..."

"Well what else can it be?" the doc asked.

"Sure, it has to be that," Ellroy admitted, anger growing in his voice at those damn kids.

Doctor Carter let his frustration loose then too. "Well, I sure as hell don't know where they are. If it wasn't some prank then what the hell happened? Where are they? They didn't just get up and *walk* the hell out of here!"

Sheriff Ellroy gulped nervously, then smiled knowing that could just not be true, but his inside gut told him something quite different. He had one of those lawman hunches again and he didn't like what it told him.

"I'll be right over," Ellroy responded, then he hung up the phone and got up from his desk. "Herman, we might have some trouble over at Doc's. Them bodies went up missing."

"Missing?"

"Come on. Let's go take a look."

Chapter 9: The Search

**OCTOR** HOWARD CARTER led Sheriff Ellroy and Deputy Sikes into the small operating room and over to the empty autopsy table.

"Last I saw them, they were laying right here. I went out for a moment to have a cigarette, like I said, and when I came back, they were gone. Gone!"

Ellroy rubbed his head, it was throbbing, the headache had returned full-force but the twisty fear in his gut and the chill running down his spine now hardly made him notice the headache at all.

Deputy Sikes just laughed nervously, forced, then grinned, "Okay, nice joke, Howie. Now go and get 'em, right now. We don't have time for this."

"No joke, Deputy, I swear," the doctor replied real serious and showing deep concern now, and maybe a bit of fear as well. After all, things like this were not supposed to happen.

"Well they just didn't get up and walk on out of here!" Sikes barked tensely, trying a bit too hard to ignore his own mounting fear and just what it might mean. That maybe—just maybe—they had actually done just that!

The sheriff and the doctor were made of sterner stuff and just shook their heads. They were coldly logical men and proud of it. Neither of them could accept that kind of foolishness. There had to be some logical explanation for this, for sure.

"Look, this is getting us nowhere," Sheriff Ellroy began, keeping calm and injecting some sanity. "Look, Howie, if this is some prank I will make that person—*whoever he might be*—rue the day, understand?"

"It's no prank, Birch, leastways not from my end. I swear it."

"Okay, so let's do a pattern search," Ellroy ordered, but he was unable to look away from that empty table for more than a moment. It compelled his attention now with it being empty. He looked around the room carefully now, and noticed some tiny droppings on the floor for the first time. A couple of small pieces of what appeared to be human remains lay upon the floor, along with some dead or dying maggots. Ellroy and the doctor looked at them carefully. The doctor gingerly collected them with tweezers and placed the material into a sterilized jar as the sheriff looked at them and couldn't help but think of the children's nursery rhyme—Hansel and Gretel. They'd left crumbs behind them in the forest so they could find their way home. Maybe these corpses—strike that—*they'd* done nothing—but maybe whoever had *taken* them, had obviously jostled them quite a bit. That had caused the corpses to leave behind little bits and pieces of their tiny body things that had fallen off—and if he followed the trail that might lead him to them. He told his theory to the doctor and his deputy.

"That's spooky, Birch," Herman Sikes said. "Hansel and Gretel, eh?"

"I noticed that too, Sheriff, but didn't know what to make of it. You think we can follow them? Track them down that way?"

"We can try," Ellroy said and began his search for tiny bits of leftover material on the floor that might lead him to his goal. There was not much to go on and the pieces were small and far between, but they were there to see if you looked carefully. He found some specks of dust and rot and began following it, with Doctor Carter and Deputy Sikes coming along behind him.

Sheriff Ellroy tried to hold down a nagging fear, a fear that kept creeping at the edges of his reason. For reason told him one thing quite plainly, but fear and his cop hunches told him something else entirely different. And having these feelings at odds with each other was never a good sign and was causing him considerable discomfort.

Reason told Ellroy that some damn kids must be playing a prank on Doc Carter and they'd soon track these leftover remains to where the bodies had been hidden. Disgusting work. Yet, his cop senses told him something entirely different, whispering to him that it was nothing like that at all — nothing within his scope of experience at all. That scared the big, blustery sheriff to his core, because it did occur to Ellroy that the girl had told him through her catatonic stupor that some maggot-infested monster killed and carried off Lamont — but he refused to believe such craziness. He had to put it out of his mind; he was a logical guy, well-grounded. So it could never be true. It was *not* true!

He heard crows outside the building in the surrounding trees cawing wildly. Frenzied, they had been disturbed by something. Most unusual this time of night, he reflected. An omen? He put the thought out of his mind and concentrated on the problem at hand.

"Come on, the trail seems to lead out here, into the hallway."

Carter and Sikes followed Ellroy warily. Sikes had now drawn his gun and when the sheriff turned around and noticed this he shook his head.

"No, Herman, put that away. You want to end up shooting me, or the doc here?"

Deputy Sikes gave a nervous grin and quickly holstered his weapon, but with obvious reluctance. Ellroy could see that his deputy was spooked. So was the doctor. Hell, so was he!

The lights were put on in the office hallway. Other offices had their doors all closed, locked shut. These included offices for Harry Davis the local dentist, Joel Swartz the foot doctor, and Linda Bramor, who was a dermatologist. It was Macedonia Village one-stop medical center shopping.

Ellroy checked the doors to each of these offices. They appeared undamaged, the locks not tampered with. Just to be sure he tried the doors, all locked as he'd expected. He continued to follow the trail—suddenly realizing that it really was a trail—so then a thought came to him of something that might just be needed if this little macabre mystery didn't clear up mighty fast.

"Come on, it leads through the hall out here to the reception area," he said, but there the trail seemed to stop. The reception area was carpeted; it was next to impossible to see the tiny remains that had fallen off the corpses there. It was next to impossible to pick up the trail now.

"I assume they went out the front door...through here," Ellroy looked at the doctor for some confirmation.

"Yes, it wasn't locked at the time."

"I guess you were still out back?"

"Yeah, so someone could have snuck in the front door here, taken the bodies and left through this way."

Ellroy nodded, went to the doors and looked at the handles, then felt them — they felt weird. He pulled his hand back and smelled his fingers. It was faint, but it was there, the smell of death. The smell of rotting flesh was upon his fingers. It was unmistakable.

"You smell it too?" Carter asked.

"You can smell it?" Ellroy replied, surprised that the doctor's sense of smell was obviously a lot keener than his own.

"Why's that smell on the door handle? What's it doing there?" Carter asked concerned now at the implication. "That could only mean ..."

"Now, Howie, let's not get ahead of ourselves here and jump to conclusions," Ellroy told his friend as he took a deep breath in an effort to relax his own growing tension. "Look, the kids probably bumped one of the corpses against the door on the way out. Just a clumsy bunch of kids. That's all it is."

"Yeah, of course, that's got to be it!" Sikes blurted with relief, almost thankfully that Ellroy had come up with that very logical explanation. God alone knew where his thoughts had been heading.

"Okay, look, we'll not find anything going about it this way. Herman, the doc said he met Jake Burlingame before, so he may be home by now. Run on down to Jake's house and have him bring back Darth Vader. Tell him we need to borrow him to sniff out something for us. But no details, okay?"

Deputy Sikes nodded and left right away. Truth be told he was thankful to be out of that building and away from whatever was going on there. He didn't like it all one bit.

Sheriff Ellroy finally looked at the doctor once his deputy had left, "Well, Howie, let's track this as far as it goes."

"Okay, I'm game if you are," Carter gulped nervously, carefully following the big sheriff.

The trail didn't prove to be much; it didn't take them very far. In fact, the trail only took them just outside the front door of the medical building onto the front steps, down the steps, and then they lost all trace of it in the grass of the front yard.

"Damn!" Carter growled in disappointment. He was hoping to clear this mess up right away then go home and put it out of his mind.

"Not too worry, once Jake brings Darth Vader, he'll track that trail and we'll get back your bodies," Ellroy said confidently.

"Okay, that seems good, Birch," the doctor replied, taking out a cigarette and lighting it a bit nervously in spite of himself.

"Those things will kill you," Ellroy told the doc with a wan smile.

"Giving medical advice now, Birch? Just don't let on to Doris about me smoking, please. I promised her I'd quit them but I have to have one from time to time. This is one of them times I surely need one."

Sheriff Ellroy nodded agreement. It sure was one of them times.

Carter took a deep drag, puffed out the smoke almost luxuriously, looked at the sheriff and gave him a dull smile.

"So what do you think?" Carter asked as they leaned up against the railing of the front of the Macedonia Parish medial building waiting for Jake and Darth Vader.

"About what?" Ellroy asked calmly, as if he hadn't a care in the world. The sheriff was a study in calm deliberation and control, or so he appeared to those around him. Ellroy allowed a slight grin; if any of the people knew how nervous he was inside, how stressed and concerned about things, he'd never be trusted to be the sheriff here.

The doc wondered if his friend was purposely being obscure.

"I mean, what do you think about this whole mess?"

"I don't know."

"Come on!"

"I'll tell you, Howie, between you and me, I don't rightly know what to believe," Ellroy allowed, rubbing his throbbing temples, annoyed that his headache was back again and impatient that the hound wasn't there yet. He wanted to clean this mess up fast so he could get down to the real business here, the murder of the two LaRontue boys. On top of everything else, he had murders to solve, dead bodies to process, he didn't need this prankster nonsense now done by some spoilt punk kids, but he was still uneasy about it all. That old cop sense nagged at the edges of his mind.

"Well?" the doc insisted.

The sheriff sighed, "I heard some strange things, got some weird feelings about this, you know?"

"Yeah, I know."

Ellroy nodded, "But I'm sure we'll get to the bottom of it all soon enough, then we'll all have a good laugh about it afterwards."

"I didn't want to say this with Herman around—he seemed spooked enough as it is—but I can't help feeling them two dead bodies weren't taken out of here."

"What do you mean?" Ellroy even dreaded to ask the question.

"I mean, Birch, I think they just got up and *walked* on out of here."

Sheriff Ellroy sighed, looked at his friend, and just shook his head laughing. Well, there it was, said out in the open now. Doc Carter had said it plain and clean and Ellroy had to admit that's the very thing that had been nagging deep down in his own mind—what he'd been fearing but unable to voice out loud. And he knew his deputy had been thinking the same damn thing too.

Ellroy took a deep thoughtful breath before he answered the doctor, "Look, strange things happen, this is Louisiana after all—but walking corpses? Come on, Howie! This ain't no low-budget voodoo, hoodoo movie, this is real life here. These things just don't happen. It's gotta be some of them damn kids. Face it, Howie, you been punked!"

Doctor Carter laughed, stubbed out his cigarette, "Guess you're right, Birch."

"You know I am."

"Well, when I catch that little son of a bitch..."

"When I catch him, Howie, he'll rue the day," Ellroy stated with a laugh.

"Still, I wish I could be as certain as you are."

"Hah, what makes you think I'm certain?"

Doctor Carter flushed a sudden nervous look at the Sheriff's face, then smiled, "Sure, that's a good one, but I know that's got to be it."

There was suddenly a loud commotion as a car pulled up.

"Look, here's Herman and he's got Jake and his dog in tow," Ellroy said in evident relief. Now he could get down to business. "Howie, look, don't mention too much about this to Jake. Let me do the talking."

The doctor nodded in agreement.

Big old Jake Burlingame came on over, said his hellos. He had his old hound dog Darth Vader on a lead chain beside him. "I hear tell you boys got two escaped zombies walking around the village and you need to track 'em down."

Ellroy looked askance at his deputy, "What the hell did you tell him?"

"Ah, I just, sorta ..."

Ellroy shook his head in anger and exasperation. "Look, Jake, Herman is just funning you, but thanks for coming. We got ourselves a situation here. Some kids from the school, more than likely, are pulling a prank on the doc here. While he was having a smoke out back with you an hour ago, they crept inside and stole two corpses he had laid out on his autopsy table. We need to find them now. You think Darth Vader can track down the scent and put us on the trail?"

"Sure thing, Birch. This here dog's got a nose just like a pure-bred hound dog," Burlingame said proudly.

"Ah, Jake, I thought Darth Vader *is* a pure-bred hound dog?" the doctor asked.

"Sure, that's what I said."

Ellroy just smiled at that and the doc just nodded as he petted the old dog. Darth Vader was a good dog, friendly and just past his prime but still a hell of a tracker with a great nose on him.

Ellroy lead Jake and his dog into the autopsy room, then Jake set his hound to work, instructing him to pick up the scent and follow the trail.

"Darth Vader's as well trained as any cadaver dog, Birch," Burlingame told the sheriff with pride. "Come on, Darth Vader, track it down! Track it down, boy!"

The dog smelled the table, the floor around the table, his large delicate nose sniffed at the few tiny specks of rotten corpse that had fallen to the floor, the maggots, the flesh and whatever he could find. He growled once deeply, sniffed again, suddenly wailed like the hound he was, then he started to bark at an area on the floor. He was loud and angry, almost ferocious. The men could see there was nothing there.

"What is it?" Ellroy asked Jake.

"Don't rightly know, Birch, never seen old Darth Vader act like that before."

Jake Burlingame held the choke collar on his hound tight and brought him closer to him as he squatted down so the two were right beside each other. "What's wrong old dog?"

Darth Vader began to squirm nervously, then he began to whine softly but with evident fear now.

"That dog's just plum scared," Sikes said, nervous himself now.

"He's not scared! That's my dog. He's just getting himself set to go to work, that's all," Burlingame blurted in defense of his hound taking the matter as if personally insulted. Then to the dog he said in a soothing voice, "Come on boy, you can do it. We can do it. Follow that scent. Take me to that scent, boy!"

Darth Vader whined like a puppy, and even growled nervously at Jake, which was unprecedented.

Jake seeing the temperament of his dog was shocked, he told him to relax, to stand down. Jake stood up and came over to Sheriff Ellroy, Deputy Sikes and the doc and shook his head sadly. "I'm sorry, boys, old Darth Vader, well, I don't rightly know what's got into him."

"I tell you that dog's just plum scared," Sikes repeated.

Jake Burlingame looked at the deputy hotly and for a moment it appeared there was going to be some hotter words, then the old dog man just nodded, "Sheriff, something's got my dog spooked, that's for sure. I ain't never seen him like that before. He's gone up against bears with nary a care, but whatever is going on here has him froze with fear. I'm sorry, but he can't help you."

Sheriff Ellroy nodded glumly, the disappointment he felt was only exceeded by the weird reaction from the dog that had truly surprised him. Ellroy knew dogs too, especially hounds. Darth Vader was a good dog. The dog had picked up a scent all right, but whatever it was it had scared the hell out of him. That never happened to any hound with living prey, and not even with dead prey — such as with a cadaver dog. And this dog had training in both of those areas of tracking. No, the dog's reaction would only be from the result of coming across something so alien, so different, that it had never encountered it before. And that dog didn't want to get anywhere near it.

That got the sheriff thinking in ways he was not happy to be thinking. So, now, whatever it was they were after, it was not living tissue, nor was it dead tissue. So then … what? The only thought that came to him was one which he had been repressing, refusing to even theorize about. Now it seemed the only alternative. Could it really be possible? Dead tissue that had somehow been reanimated? He got that chill running down his spine again even as he had the thought. What had his deputy told Jake? He'd said they were looking for zombies.

Zombies?

Chapter 10: The Search Expands

 **HERIFF** Birch Ellroy shook his head to clear the confusion, looked at the men around him and laughed nervously. The doc seemed more concerned than ever now about what had happened. Ellroy's deputy, Herman Sikes, looked more nervous than ever, and Jake the dog man seemed infernally curious. Darth Vader stood tall and firm but steadfastly refused to move from his master's side. The dog stared at the empty autopsy table and gave low menacing growls.

"Well, Jake, thanks for coming on down. Herman, why don't you run Jake and his dog back home. I'll meet you later at the office."

"Sure thing, Birch," Sikes said, relieved to get out of there.

Once they were alone Doctor Carter took out another cigarette. "What the hell is going on here, Birch?"

"I don't know," Ellroy said softly.

Two loud gun blasts got the attention of the men. The doctor dropped his cigarette and Ellroy drew his sidearm.

"What the hell was that?"

"Shotgun, two blasts," Ellroy stated firmly. "Stay here, I've got to check it out."

"No way! I'm coming with you."

There was no time to argue, "Okay, just stay behind me and be quiet."

Ellroy knew where the sound had come from, one of the houses across the street and down the block. He ran as fast as he could, soon reaching the house that he believed to be the location of the shots. It was unmistakable now, the lights were all on, a lot of people outside on the lawn screaming bloody murder. It was total chaos.

Ellroy ran up to the house winded but ready for action. There he saw Loyola Richards standing on the porch. She was covered in blood, hysterical and raving about some "things" that had killed everyone in the house and then eaten them!

Ellroy couldn't calm her down, couldn't get any sense out of her, so he quickly passed her on to the doctor to take care of. Then he entered the house alone with his weapon drawn and ready. He passed through the screen door and walked straight into a nightmare.

"What the hell!"

There was blood everywhere. The floor, the walls, the stairway, the entire first floor looked like a bloody tornado had hit it. Furniture was broken, everything had been tossed around, paintings were ripped from the walls and smashed on the floor. Everything seemed broken or trashed and seemed coated with a thin spray of fresh blood.

Ellroy was shaken by the scene and pointed his .45 to take a quick scan of the ground floor. He went room by room, searching quickly but thoroughly. He cleared the first floor. There was no one there, no perp, no body, no victim. Then he looked up the stairs at the second floor landing. So far he had not seen anyone or heard anything. He listened for sounds from above but heard nothing. With so much blood everywhere, he was surprised he couldn't find any bodies yet. That was just damn strange.

It was also inconceivable to ever see this kind of mindless violence in Macedonia Parish. Nothing like this ever happened here.

Ellroy wondered just what the hell he was walking into. He steeled his nerves. Gone now was his headache as well as the chills that had run down his spine, it had all been replaced by a dark sense of impending doom. No, not doom—evil. He shuddered involuntarily as he realized that is exactly what he felt, an overwhelming sense of evil, then he took another step forward.

He was sweating bullets from the heat and tension, his mouth was dry as a desert. He swallowed hard as he tried to focus his determination, and then began to walk up the stairway to see what he would find on the second floor.

The home Loyola Richards owned was used by her as a boarding house for some of the local working men. There were four small bedrooms upstairs with four male tenants.

Ellroy gingerly went up the creaking steps. He watched carefully, praying the noise did not alert any lurking killer, a killer who might be lying in wait for him. Outside he could still hear the Richards woman screaming wildly and he thought he heard the word "zombie" again, but he couldn't be sure. The lady had to be crazy with terror. She'd obviously seen the murder, or murders, or whatever had happened here, and been traumatized by it. But whatever had happened here, he had not discovered yet—but it surely wasn't zombies—but it could be some kind of mass murder! He moved slowly, guardedly, his gun out and ready. He knew that a big crowd would have gathered outside the house by now, that the EMS guys from the Macedonia Volunteer Fire Department would be arriving any second, but all the blood would put them off from entering the house until he called an all clear on the crime scene.

Right now, nothing was clear.

Ellroy heard the siren of a fire engine on the way. Then he looked up and saw the pool of blood on the upstairs landing and the body of one of the victims. He recognized the man from around the village. It was Herb Storm, a tenant and laborer, like the other men who lived in this house.

The sheriff moved closer, carefully pointing his .45 as he scanned the landing and the doorways for any attacker lying in wait. He knew the murderer might still be present so he had to be on the alert. He walked over to the body, gave the man a quick glance. Storm was obviously dead. The man's face was contorted in the worst vision of fear the sheriff had ever seen this side of some gore-fest horror film. It was uncanny.

Herb Storm was obviously very dead. And the man had died hard, blood was all over the hallway, and it looked like his throat had been shot out with a shotgun, or... maybe even cut out? With something sharp and jagged. Maybe... teeth? No, that just could not be, Ellroy thought. He'd have to show this to the doc to get his opinion. It had to be from some kind of knife. Maybe one of those cooking knives with the serrated edges?

The sheriff left Storm's body and continued his investigation of the murder scene. He discovered three more male bodies, the other three renters, each one of whom had the same kind of damage to their neck. It was as if their throats had been chewed or eaten. It was chilling.

One of the men, Brax Jones, had a double-barrel shotgun in his room lying on the floor. Ellroy picked it up and saw that it had recently been fired. This was the gun he had heard. Ellroy noted that the blasts had hit a portion of the doorway, blowing a hole into the doorjamb and spraying buckshot all over the wall. Jones had died just as hard as the others, but at least he'd tried to fight off what had attacked him. Not very successfully, that was evident, but he had put up some form of resistance, getting off two blasts from that shotgun.

Ellroy noticed something else on the floor by the wall. He wondered what it could be. He carefully stooped down to pick it up, holding it in his free hand. He looked at it more clearly wondering just what the hell it was. It seemed to move, white nodules were all over it. Suddenly he felt nauseous and screamed wildly, instantly dropping the thing from his fingers, rubbing his hand furiously on his pants leg trying to get it clean. What he had found had been part of a human finger, a long dead and rotting finger, with maggots crawling all over it.

Ellroy suddenly grew dizzy and knew that he had to get out of there right away.

Chapter 11: The Brothers

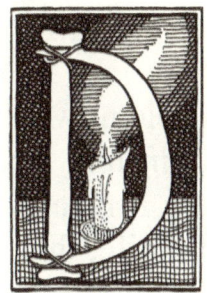 OC CARTER LOOKED LIKE HELL; they all looked like hell. He'd seen to Loyola Richards, the only survivor of the murder spree, or whatever it was that had happened in her house. She'd been so traumatized by the event she was unable to speak coherently about what had happened. She just kept mumbling over and over again one word: "zombies," but that was quite enough.

By now panic was beginning to spread through the village of Macedonia Parish. Trudy Nelson of the *Post* had arrived at the scene and had taken some photos of the devastation, then tried to get some statements from the neighbors and the sheriff.

"This is an ongoing police investigation," was all Sheriff Birch Ellroy told her mechanically in his best bureaucratic policese tone, "so I can not comment at this time."

"Oh come on, Birch!" Trudy glared. "Enough of the cop spiel."

Ellroy just shook his head and walked over to where the doctor and his deputy were talking. Deputy Herman Sikes had finally arrived on the scene from dropping Jake and his dog home.

"So what's the score?" Ellroy asked tersely.

"We got four dead, Birch; Herb Storm, Brax Jones, Bobby Fell and Ivan Garcia," Sikes told him glumly, the shock showed easily on the young deputy's face.

Doctor Carter added, "They appear to have all been killed by massive lacerations to the throat, severing the carotid artery and with great loss of blood."

"So what do we have as the murder weapon? A knife? Razor?" Ellroy asked, almost hopefully.

Doctor Carter gulped nervously, not even able now to hold back the thoughts he had brewing within him by what he had seen, and by what he now knew it meant. "No, Birch, their throats were not cut by any knife, they were ripped out, and it appears that it was done by teeth. They had also been chewed."

"Chewed?" Ellroy muttered softly as his face blanched. He hardly knew what to say about that but looked at his friend's face as if he had not heard him correctly.

"I'm not kidding," the doctor added ominously. "There are teeth marks on all the bodies — corpses."

Ellroy thought it through logically. Okay, there had to be some reasonable explanation.

"By what then?" Ellroy asked sharply, "Some animal? A bear?" However, even as he uttered the words he felt they came out as mere shadows in the air in front of him, false and hopelessly wrong words without real meaning.

It was left to Ellroy's deputy, Herman Sikes, almost hysterical himself with fear, to put what they all felt into words. "Why do you refuse to believe it, Birch? The old lady said it plain enough. It's zombies! We've got zombies running loose here!"

"Easy, Herman," Ellroy ordered sharply.

"Jake's dog smelled 'em, wouldn't go near 'em. You know it as well as I do!"

Doctor Carter cleared his throat, looking from Sikes to Ellroy, "Birch, I think we have to face the facts here."

"What facts, Howie? Zombies? Come on!"

"No, you come on. Wake up, Birch!" the doc demanded.

Birch Ellroy reacted to the words like a cold slap in the face. He nodded gravely, then said, "All right. Maybe I've been denying it all along, trying to tamp down my own feelings and what my cop sense was telling me. But zombies? Come on, Howie!"

"Well something... Maybe just something like that, yes," the doc said seriously. "Look, I checked the sample you found in the house upstairs, that finger. It belonged to one of my missing corpses, one of the LaRontue Brothers."

"So it *was* them?" Ellroy said in anger at this verification of his worst fears. The things had been in the house and attacked the four men.

If this was true—dammit, and it was—that meant Macedonia Parish had two dead monsters running rampant through the village killing people... and eating their flesh! Ellroy's mind reeled at the thought. While his police training told him it just could not be true—that this just could not be happening—evidence told him plainly that it was happening. How could it be? The realization turned his thoughts quickly to his wife, Sue and his son, Tommy, both at home, alone. What if these things broke into his own house? What if they went after his family?

"Look, Herman, you and the doc finish up here," Ellroy said softly, much more introspective now. "I gotta go home for a few minutes, check on my family."

"Good idea, Birch," Sikes added. "Now you see what I been trying to tell ya."

Birch Ellroy only nodded.

Doctor Carter added, "I'm having Doris come stay with me here. I think we should all stay together. I'll see you when you get back."

"Yeah, then we'll find a way out of this," Ellroy replied in a more determined tone. For the first time in his life as a cop his confidence had been shaken but he would not give up. He would never give up! Even as a New Orleans cop, even after all he'd had to deal with during Katrina, he had not seen anything like what he'd just seen in that woman's house.

What concerned Ellroy most now was that what was happening might only be the tip of the iceberg of these strange events. As a cop he'd stood up to evil men — gang leaders, criminals, serial killers, and mobsters — and never blinked. He'd stood up to Katrina, the wild wrath of berserk Mother Nature, and was one of the few New Orleans cops who had stayed at his post and done his duty to help the people. But this was different. This wasn't like any of the things he'd ever had to deal with in the past. This was something entirely new and something not logical...not even natural. It felt like something supernatural and...supremely evil.

"Doc, see to it the bodies are taken out of the house and placed in your morgue freezer. I want you to give them a thorough going over first thing tomorrow morning," Ellroy ordered on his way out. "I'll see you later."

On his way to his Jeep he ran into Trudy Nelson again and tried to keep the frustration out of his reaction to her questions.

"Birch, what the hell is going on? I keep hearing talk about...zombies? Is that true?"

"I don't know, yes, I think it is. Look, you need to run a story in the morning paper telling everyone to lock their doors and stay inside their homes. They should report to me if they see anything suspicious. I have to go now," he said rapidly, trying to give her the brush, as he quickly got into his Jeep. "I have to go now, Trudy."

He drove away without another word and raced for home.

Chapter 12: Chaos Grows

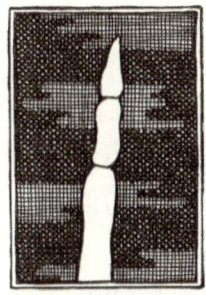T WAS LATE when Sheriff Birch Ellroy got home but all the lights in the house were on. That got him nervous and alert. He didn't want to think about what could be wrong.

"Please God, don't make it be anything bad," he whispered as he lurched his Jeep into the driveway.

Then he saw his neighbor, Buck Toler, sitting on his front porch holding an AK-47 in his lap. The man looked scared but damn serious.

"Buck?" Ellroy shouted, he walked quickly towards his own home. "What's going on here?"

"Heard all about them zombies, Birch. I'm just posting guard. You'd best get inside and see to Sue and Tommy. They're scared, everyone here is."

"I will, thanks."

Ellroy ran into his house. He was met by his wife Susan in the living room. She held a gun in her hands, one of his older .45s. He noticed she still had the safety on. She put the gun down and ran into his arms.

"Oh, Birch! My God, you're alive!" she cried wild with terror, wet streaming tears of joy and fear.

"Where's Tommy?"

"I told him to lock himself in his room," she said, hugging her husband tightly like she'd never want to let him go. Then she spoke nervously, quickly, "I heard what happened at Mrs. Richards place. It's all over the news, people on the street are already talking about it. Is it really a serial killer? Or … the other thing? I heard … you know? Can it be?"

"It's not any serial killer, Sue," he said grimly.

"Are you serious? What does that mean then? I heard the word zombies, but it just can't be … Can it? I heard four men were killed and that two dead bodies just got up and walked away from Doctor Carter's morgue. How the hell can that happen? Is any of this true, Birch? What the hell is going on?"

"I don't know, Sue. Look, get Tommy, we're leaving here now. You're coming to stay with me."

"At the Sheriff's office and jail?" she asked astonished.

"I don't know, but wherever I am, I want you both with me all the time now. We'll set up something, a central command post. I'm not clear on everything just yet. I have to call in the State Police, get some help out here," he said forcefully, nervously. It did not give her confidence to see him like that. He was never unsure of himself, now he was almost frantic and barely holding himself in check. "Now get Tommy. Pack light and fast. Bring food. And that spare .45. We don't have much time."

It was the longest night in the history of Macedonia Parish. No one slept a wink, everyone feared for their lives, and the lives of their loved ones, as the rumors of vicious murders spread like wildfire. Whether it was by some biker gang, a serial killer or even zombies, it made no difference to most people at that point because by then the fear had spread into every home throughout the small village and then to people in the outlying farms.

Sheriff Birch Ellroy set up a command post at the Central High School up on Thomas Street. Local Red Cross and church folk brought in cots and food and everyone in the village, and those in the rural areas of the parish, were told to get to the high school as quickly as they could. They were told to bring any weapons they had — but not loaded.

The State Police had been called and Ellroy had been assured help would be arriving by the morning. He didn't dare mention the word "zombies" to the commander, he just told him about the mass murder of the four men and that there apparently was some kind of serial killer or mass murderer loose in Macedonia Parish. The commander assured him that help would arrive soon.

An emergency had been declared. People kept trucking into the high school from the village and later on in the evening from the surrounding farms as the word spread. Ellroy put Trudy Nelson in charge of keeping track of things there. The mayor was only too happy to step back and allow the sheriff to run things in this situation.

"I need you to make a list of all the people in Macedonia Parish," Ellroy told her quickly. "Then check them off as they come in. I want everyone here and we need to keep track of our people to be sure if they are here or not. I know a lot of the old people and some of those who live in the rural areas will have trouble getting transportation. Maybe you can get Jack Burlingame and his sons to help out, they can drive around and do some pick ups?"

"I'm sure Jake would help," Trudy said, too awed by the job put upon her to even think of what it all meant. Her entire world was falling apart before her eyes. Sleepy, rural Macedonia Parish was turning into hell on earth. "I can get a list of all parish residents at the Village Hall. I think we could get everyone here in a day or so."

"Make it faster. I don't know if we've got that much time," Ellroy said quickly. He had a growing fear that he was rapidly losing control of the situation and that things were a lot more unstable than they appeared to be. Like an iceberg, it was said you only saw the 10 percent that was above the water. If that was true, there was a lot more going on underneath than he even suspected.

Ellroy was relieved that Sue and Tommy were at the high school now and felt they were safer there than being alone at home without him.

He talked to Tommy in an effort to calm his son, but the boy seemed to have the situation well in hand. In fact, he seemed to know all about zombies from TV, films, even books.

"This isn't TV or a movie, Tommy," Birch tried to explain to his son with a wry grin.

"Don't worry, Pa, you'll get them. The thing is if a person is killed by a zombie they become a zombie too. So you gotta watch out for anyone bitten. Even scratches can cause a person to turn. I'll tell you how to fight 'em, too. Everyone knows you gotta shoot them in the head, that will stop 'em, but only for a while. The way to kill 'em for good is to set them on fire. That's the only way to stop them for good. Gasoline is good for that, Pa," Tommy said seriously.

Birch smiled, messed his son's hair lovingly, but looked at the boy in a new way too. The kid was right, he seemed to know his stuff, and his information might prove useful — even if it was taken from TV or movies. What the hell, if it worked, it worked!

"Okay, son, thanks for the advice," Birch told him.

"Don't worry, Pa, I know we'll come through this okay," Tommy said.

Birch kissed his wife and son and then left them with Trudy. He was thankful that Trudy was coordinating things at the school and knew that Sue would help her. Between the two of them they would have things soon well in hand. Now he had to leave Sue, he had a lot of things that needed to be done. First he had to get over to the medical building and talk to Doctor Carter to learn what he'd discovered regarding the bodies of the four murdered men at the Richards house.

Chapter 13: The Doctor

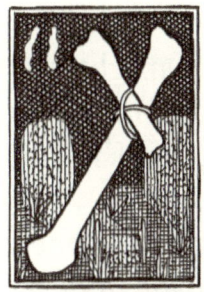**OU** SEEM TO BE THE MAN who never sleeps," Ellroy said as he walked into Doctor Carter's office.

"One could say the same of you, Birch. I think it's five A.M., it'll be sunup soon. What a night. Ready for a new day?"

"No, not really. You check out those dead guys?"

"Yeah, come inside and take a look at them."

The two men walked out of the doc's office into the back operating room he used for autopsies and also as a makeshift morgue for the parish.

"By the way, did you bring Doris to the high school yet?"

"Yeah, she was reluctant at first. She was sleeping when I burst in on her at one o'clock in the morning. She went to sleep early and hadn't heard any of the news — like a lot of folks, I expect. It was a shock to her. She's down there now. What about Sue and that boy of yours?"

"They're there too. I set up Trudy Nelson as coordinator. That'll be our command center. I think she'll be good at getting everything organized, she's got a knack that way. We need everyone rounded up and brought to the high school asap, and keeping Trudy busy will also keep her out of my hair," Ellroy said with a grin. "That should keep her busy."

"Trudy is a good organizer," Carter smiled. "Any news yet on the State Police or the Feds?"

"No Feds, they see it as a local matter. The FBI in New Orleans says their resources are spread too thin, but if it gets more serious … "

"Sure, if the body count goes up high enough… Or if there is significant media interest?"

"Yeah, you know the game, well then they might just do a drop in. I didn't mention anything about zombies to them, or to the State Police. I may be crazy, but I'm not stupid."

Carter laughed shaking his head. "I see. I think that's a good idea. You know, I'm not partial to the federal government anyway. Not many people in these parts are since Katrina, and lately that damn oil spill that screwed up the Gulf waters … Well, let's just say the word secession hadn't been as popular around here since the Civil War."

"The War Between the States," Ellroy corrected the doctor with a grin.

"So I heard," Carter smirked, then he got serious and led the sheriff into the back room. They entered as the doc put on the light. There they saw four male bodies—or what was left of them—laid out on shiny aluminum tables.

"Well, here they are," Carter said with mock flourish of his right arm.

"So what exactly do we have here?" Ellroy began, startled by the mess that was all that was left of the dead men.

"Nothing good, I can tell you. Each of the men was killed by having his throat ripped out, then chewed. I think, eaten. I found what I was looking for, Birch. Evidence of teeth marks."

"Teeth marks? Please tell me it was a bear? Or maybe we have a coyote loose?"

"No, it was human teeth marks on all of them."

"All right," and Sheriff Ellroy didn't say another word. He was busy thinking a mile a second now, wondering what the hell was going on in his parish and what the hell was he going to do about it?

"Sorry to have to tell you this, Birch, but I know you want me to give it to you straight. I knew it was what you might be afraid of."

"Yeah."

"I don't know what the implication means, but I sure as hell don't like it. Makes me almost wish this was the result of some damn serial killer, a Bundy or a Gacy, even. That at least might make things much simpler in the end," Carter said, speaking grim truth.

Sheriff Ellroy agreed, while he stared at the four corpses in front of him. Four men. He didn't really know any of them that well. Their lives snuffed out in an orgy of brutal violence he'd never seen the likes of before in his life. He examined the neck wounds on each of them. My God, what a terrible way to die! He knew the men had still been alive when this had been done to them, it had been done pre-mortem. That's what really got to him, the sheer animal ferocity of the killings. He shivered when his thoughts turned to his wife and son, and the other people of the village, and imagined something like this happening to them.

"So what's next?" Doctor Carter asked breaking in on the sheriff's dire forebodings.

Ellroy shrugged, still staring at the body of the first victim he'd encountered in the upstairs hall of the Richards house. What was his name? Herb Storm. He looked at the body closely, fixating on that ghastly neck wound, and then that face, still contorted in agonized fear. It was obvious the man had been taken by complete surprise by his killer. Had that killer really been Lamont LaRontue? Or the other brother, Amos? Those two bodies he had discovered entwined so tightly in a grave at LaRontue Mansion. Had one of them — those dead things — really done this?

"Birch?"

Ellroy's eyes were still locked onto the man on the metal slab when his eyes suddenly did a double take.

What was that? He looked hard, shocked now.

What had he just seen?

Had it been … movement?

Ellroy knew he'd been run ragged with this case and the lack of sleep, but still …

There is was again!

"Doc?"

"Yeah, so I wanted to ask you, what do you want to do next?"

"Doc?"

"Yeah, Birch?"

"That thing moved!"

"Moved? Are you sure?" Carter asked, his eyes darting at the corpse sharply, getting closer to examine it intently.

"I'm telling you that thing moved! I saw it!"

"You're tired, Birch, that's all."

"No, I don't think so," Ellroy told him and drew his .45 and took off the safety.

"No need for that in here," Carter said carefully.

"I tell you, I know what I saw, Howie!"

"All right," the doctor said, examining the corpse more closely. "This one seems … "

Both men suddenly froze.

What was left of the body of Herb Storm began to twitch, arms and legs slowly moved, head lolled back and forth on a torn neck stub. Both men could not believe what they were seeing. It was as if the dead man was trying to get up from the table.

The other three bodies on the tables instantly began to show signs of movement now as well. It was as if they had all just decided to come back to life on their own, twitching and shaking and twisting.

"Holy shit!" Carter barked in fear, jumping away from the wiggling dead things, totally amazed as he looked at them with growing terror and disgust.

"Please tell me that's from some type of normal post-mortem muscle contractions, Howie," Ellroy blurted hopefully, but cold fear clouded his eyes and grew as they transfixed on the twitching things on the tables in front of him.

"No way, Birch. That is nothing I've ever seen before."

"They're alive?" Ellroy was shocked. It was incomprehensible, but all his disbelief now melted away. He took a deep breath and aimed his .45 at the corpses in front of him but he was not sure exactly what to do. Should he just shoot them? Should he kill them? Would a bullet even kill them? They were already dead, weren't they, so what would killing them again do? Then he thought about what his son Tommy had told him about zombies...

"They're not alive, Birch, but they are ... moving ... They are somehow reanimating right before our eyes," the doctor told him fearfully.

"Son of a bitch!" Ellroy shouted, stepping back in terror now, for a split second he even forgot he was still pointing his .45 at the creatures. "They *are* alive!"

"They're coming back and they're going to get up and do just what the other ones did, Birch. You have to stop them."

"I have to stop them? What the hell can I do?"

Doctor Carter moved back looking to the sheriff to do something.

Sheriff Ellroy nodded grimly, it took him a moment to fully accept the facts of the situation, that dead squirming corpses on those tables were coming back to life before his very eyes. He knew what he had to do now. His son Tommy had given him the idea. Before the four things were able to fully reanimate he brought his .45 up to the head of each of the corpses and put a slug into the brain of each of the four bodies. Four shots rang out. The zombie things shuddered and then fell back upon the table apparently lifeless and still. Were they dead? Finally dead? Who could tell? But at least they had stopped moving.

"Thank God!" Ellroy muttered. He was sweating rivers, he was soaked with nervous cold clammy sweat but he added grimly, "At least we know a bullet in the head kills them, Doc."

"Do we, Birch?" Doctor Carter asked, his body shaking fearfully at what he had just witnessed. It went against all of his scientific training, all logical thought and nature. He'd never have thought this could be possible if he had not witnessed it himself. Those dead men had actually come back to life!

"You mean you think … ?" Ellroy replied, holstering his .45 while he kept his eyes sharply on the now motionless corpses. "You think they could … ? You know? Come back alive again?"

"I don't know," Carter answered seriously, starring at the motionless corpses. "Maybe. They did it once, why not again?"

"Then we burn 'em! Burn the sons of bitches, doc!" Ellroy ordered. "That should do it!"

Carter nodded agreement. It seemed like a good idea and who knew, it might even work. It might even be final. He said, "Makes sense, Birch. If we burn 'em and they have no bodies left to 'em, seems to me they could never reanimate."

The two men wheeled the gurneys out the back door of the medical building and carried the four bodies out back. They made a pile of the four in an open space on the grass. Ellroy went back to his Jeep for one of the five-gallon cans of gasoline he always carried for emergencies. This certainly qualified. Then he poured the gas over the pile of bodies, soaking them thoroughly, pouring it all until the can was empty. Then he lit a match and set the fire. It blazed like mad, giving off a thick horrid black smoke odor, the smell of the charnel pit.

"Sorry boys," Ellroy said in grim humor to the four flaming masses of flesh, "but this is Macedonia Parish and once you're dead, you just gotta stay dead. Please."

"Amen," Carter added softly.

Chapter 14: Battle Ground

**O** WHAT IS OUR NEXT STEP, Birch?" Carter asked the sheriff once they had seen to the fire and were sure it had done its job. They were now back inside the building in Carter's office.

"We've got to find those two — creatures — the LaRontue brothers—before they attack anyone else, or pass on whatever they have in them that will create more of those ... things ... "

" ... Zombies?" Carter finished the thought. He knew it was a word the sheriff did not want to use. He didn't like it as well. "It must be some kind of bacteria, or perhaps some virus they picked up in the gravesite, then they pass it on when they eat the flesh of a living person."

"Yeah, I guess you're right about that. That, at least makes sense to me. I guess," Ellroy said, though none of this really made any sense to him at all. It just terrified him and all he could think of was his wife and son.

Carter shook his head, "With all the troubles in this here world—and Lord knows we have seen our share in this country and this state—you'd think we'd get a break on crap like this and be the last ones to have something like this thrown in our laps."

Ellroy patted his friend on his back with affection, "When it rains, it pours, Howie."

"Yeah, you don't have to remind me. So tomorrow we start going on the hunt for the LaRontue's?"

Ellroy checked his watch and smiled grimly, it was near 7 A.M., Wednesday morning. "Yep, it's been a long night, Howie. You know what? It's Wednesday morning now. It's already *tomorrow*."

Carter sighed, "So it is."

"Well, let's get started then. Those State Police boys should show up soon."

"That's good to hear, Birch, we can use all the help we can get."

The call came into his cell phone. It was his deputy, Herman Sikes and he was near frantic.

"Birch! You there?"

"Yeah, Herman, what's up?"

"I was out here with Jake Burlingame and his sons, Barney and Burl. They've been doing pick ups for Trudy over to the high school. The Carmody family never came in. Trudy called them and they never answered so she sent Jake to pick them up. Once he got here Jake called me. I was on my way over to meet him and his sons..."

"Okay, so what's the problem?" Ellroy asked feeling a sense of impending doom quickly rushing in upon him, wishing his deputy would get to the point. "So what happened?"

There was a momentary pause, "I'd better let Jake tell you what he found. I'm off on another call. Things are hopping all over."

Ellroy shook his head in exasperation, "All right then, put Jake on."

"I got him on the other line, hold on, I'll switch you."

"Okay, Herman, and keep me informed."

Suddenly Jake Burlingame's rough voice came on the phone, "Birch, it's Jake here."

"Yeah, Jake, what's going on there?"

"That's just it..."

"What's just it?"

"It's a mess, man, we found them, they're all dead. Bloody hell it was too, young Alice and both her parents... I never seen nothing like it before let me tell you... Leastways not until they came back to life..."

"Oh, shit!"

"Yeah, you got that right! They scared me outta my wits! They were all set and dead—then all of a sudden-like all three came back to life. Scared the bloody hell out of me and my two sons. We was loading their bodies onto the flatbed of my truck when they all of a sudden started twitching and turning, then moving real spry. At first we just watched them, you know? We couldn't believe what we was seeing. We was amazed! Hell, we was scared shitless! Well, they became spry and full of gumption real fast. They was looking for trouble. Birch, they attacked us! So we had to shoot 'em."

Ellroy was alarmed. He left the doc and ran over to his Jeep and started it up. Then he peeled out and headed over to the Carmody place before it was too late.

He still held his phone to his ear as he drove, "Look, I'm coming over right now, Jake. Tell me this, when you shot them, did they go down?"

"Sure enough they did! But, ah … something ain't right here. They was dead, but they wouldn't stay dead very long—we had to kill them a second time."

"Did you shoot them in the head?" Birch asked as he gunned his Jeep down the street.

"No, mostly full body gut and chest shots, but they went down fast enough."

"Damn!"

"Damn is right, Birch! What the hell is going on here?"

"I'm on my way over. Listen, don't do anything or go anywhere, but keep a sharp eye on them. If they come back alive shoot them in the head. Got that? In the head! And Jake, you got a can of gasoline?"

"Yeah, but… I mean… You think they could come back… again?"

Jake's voice suddenly stopped talking and Ellroy could hear gun shots.

Then the phone went dead.

No, not dead, it had been dropped to the ground. It was still on, and he could hear faint background noise, screams, more shooting, more screams…

"Jake?" Ellroy shouted. "Jake, answer me!"

There was no response but Ellroy could hear terrified screams and gun shots far off in the background.

Jake Burlingame dropped his phone in terror once he saw the dead things his sons had been hauling into the back of his pickup come back alive and attack his boys. For a crucial moment he stood in utter shock, and so did his sons. Terror had gripped them all.

Jake then pulled out his gun and got off six rounds at the things, but not before they had been at both his sons. Jake saw that Burl and Barney were bleeding from half a dozen wounds. Bites. Teeth bites!

"The damn thing bit my finger right off, Pa!" Burl shouted in rage and terror, trying to staunch the bleeding with his shirt as he tried to help his brother.

The other son, Barney, looked worse.

"Get in the truck boys, I'm taking you to Doc Carter right away. But first, dump those zombie bastards out of my truck and get me that shotgun. I'm going to blast what's left of them freaks to Kingdom Come."

The two big cars carried four men each; six Louisiana State Troopers and two F.B.I. agents from the New Orleans office. They only stopped when they came upon the dead bodies.

They had been sent in response to a call from the local sheriff about a serial killer running amok in Macedonia Parish. Now, lo and behold, no sooner had they crossed the Parish line out here in the middle of rural nowhere, than they had come upon two freshly butchered corpses lying in the middle of the state highway.

"Man and a woman, looks like," Agent Vance Fields said tightly, because it looked like a very harsh killing. He was in the front seat of the first car and had a better view of the carnage than the others. He was the agent in charge. "Well, pull over and let's take a look at 'em."

They did just that. The two cars pulled over to the side of the eerily empty highway and parked so they were out of the way of any approaching vehicles. However, no cars or trucks were approaching from either direction. Come to think of it, Agent Fields had not seen a car or a truck for quite a while since they'd entered the parish. Even out on a rural highway like this that was quite unusual.

The six troopers and two F.B.I. men got out of their cars and walked over to the corpses to investigate their strange discovery.

"What a mess!" one of the younger state cops said in evident disgust.

"Most unusual," another man said to the FBI guy as he pulled out a cigar and looked at the bodies. He did not light his cigar.

"Damn sick if you ask me," another remarked shaking his head with shock. "Look at them!"

The bodies were very bloody, they had obviously been brutally assaulted; their murder had been vicious in the extreme.

One of the troopers, a rookie from Biloxi, fought to hold back from vomiting just as one of his more seasoned brothers, in sheer terror at the sight before him, suddenly let loose with a projectile discharge of vomit containing that morning's earlier breakfast of pancakes at IHOP. The other seven lawmen looked away, each trying to maintain their precarious control over their own stomach reaction. Each one doing their best not to get a whiff of the brutal vomit smell that would make them lose their breakfasts too. No one said a word about their comrade puking. At any moment any one of them could upchuck just as easily now by what they were viewing, and they all knew it.

"Look here, these two been eaten," one of the troopers pointed out fearfully, wondering just what the hell kind of freaky killer they might be dealing with out here. "These bodies look like they been chewed on, boss."

"Wild animals, most likely, they're all around out here in the boonies," Agent Fields told them confidently. He could feel the terror in the air, knew it was affecting his team. These troopers were tough, but he doubted they'd ever run across this kind of sheer butchery before, not even in most serial killer cases. He repeated confidently, "Wild animals, most likely."

Those were the last words Agent Fields uttered before he and his men found themselves suddenly set upon by the two creatures in front of them who were supposed to be lying dead on the road. They were not dead. They were now active and full of energy, power and violence.

The attack on the lawmen was sudden and ravenous. Before the men could even draw their weapons vicious bites were taken out of their flesh. The troopers were stunned, in utter shock really; they'd never encountered anything like this before, and each man fought to pull the creatures from his comrades, pull them away from their brothers, but the things seemed to possess superhuman strength. They also seemed to have a brutality and ravenous hunger that was unimaginable. The things had already inflicted serious bites to six of Agent Field's team before one of the troopers was able to free an arm to draw his sidearm and began blasting the creatures to hell.

"Die you bastards!" the trooper shouted in terror.

The other men were able to draw their guns now and began pumping a fusillade of lead into the two creatures. Dozens of rounds entered the things, tearing them apart, blowing pieces off them, but still they continued with their attack. The troopers emptied their guns into the things, and as more and more slugs tore into them, the things finally seemed to slow down, weaken, then suddenly drop down to the highway tarmac.

Apparently dead.

Finally!

"Damn!" Agent Fields muttered. His gun was empty.

"That put them down!" the young trooper from Biloxi shouted; he was nursing a particularly vicious bite, as were all his comrades.

"Freakin' bastards!" another trooper remarked in grim fear to his buddies, nursing a bloody wound to his neck with a handkerchief. "Them damn things bite worse than a AC-DC prostitute crack whore. I sure hope I don't catch nothing."

Another trooper cried out in panic, "You just got bit by a dead thing! We all did!"

"Shut up! All of you!" Agent Fields barked. "I'm calling for backup. We need help right away."

He heard no complaints on that score but he knew it would be hours, if not days, before any help arrived. Meanwhile he had wounded men to attend to.

"They got a hospital in this Macedonia Parish?" Fields' partner asked his chief.

"Don't know, John," Fields replied in a detached tone, trying to focus his mind on what had just happened. What, in fact, had just happened? Well, if he wasn't crazy or this wasn't some mass hallucination, they'd just been viciously attacked by dead bodies that had suddenly come back to life? And they'd taken a real ass kicking in the bargain. All eight of them were bleeding from various bite wounds, cuts, or scratches.

"I think they got a doctor," someone spoke up. "I'm sure they got a doctor, at least, they gotta have one. Right?"

"Well, we'd better head there first, before we see the sheriff. You want to report this back to New Orleans, Agent Fields?"

Agent Vance Fields thought about that. "I'll report back to New Orleans right away — as soon as I figure out what to tell them about this. Right now let's get to a doctor and then coordinate this with the local sheriff. Come on now boys, let's load up these bodies — what's left of them — and then get the hell out of here."

"Load them up?" a trooper asked, repulsed by the very remains of the things. He'd need gloves and a bag, maybe even a shovel to do it properly.

"Evidence, Jimmy. It's all evidence now. Come on, get them loaded into the trunks, one body in each car."

Chapter 15: Macedonia Parish

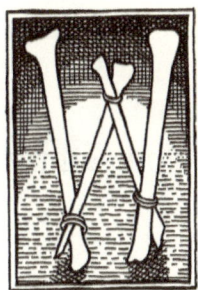**EDNESDAY** WAS ALREADY TURNING OUT to be far worse than the day before and it was still only early morning. It appeared it would be a long day.

Sheriff Birch Ellroy feared mightily for what this day might hold for him and his people, for now he knew that his greatest fear—that this damn zombie thing was real—was true and it was spreading. He raced his Jeep over to the Carmody house with that dark thought shadowing his mind.

He got there quickly and everything there looked quiet. He drove down the street and parked. There were no people on the street, and there seemed to be no one in their homes as far as he could tell. Most of the people of course had gone by now, either safe at the high school or just packed up and drove to New Orleans or out Texas way. He knew some could be hiding inside their houses, fearful and suspicious, afraid to come out. He couldn't blame them. He looked around but didn't see anyone. He didn't see his deputy, Herman Sikes, or Herman's patrol car either. That was weird. What got him even more concerned was that he didn't see hide nor hair of Jake Burlingame and his sons. Nor any bodies belonging to the Carmody family laying in the street.

"Dammit! Where the hell is everyone?" Ellroy took out his cell, called his deputy.

Sikes answered right away. "Yeah, boss?"

"Where are you?"

"Out on Highway 25. I got a call about a problem at Spring Creek bridge. Elmer Walker has a farm out that way you know, and he told me he saw two State Police cars driving wildly. When they came to the bridge they just went over it, hit the river bed down below and burst into flames."

"State Police cars? You sure?"

"That's what Elmer told me. Birch, didn't you call for help from the State Police last night?"

"Yes I did."

"Oh, man!"

"Check it out, okay. Let me know what you find out, and Herman, where the hell are Jake Burlingame and his sons — and the Carmody bodies?"

"Don't know, they were there when I left to answer this call. Everything was in order when I left. They were taking out the Carmodys and putting them in the back of Jake's truck."

"Look, Herman, I gotta go, I got another call. Please be careful and let me know what you find. If any of those bodies are still alive, shoot 'em in the head and then set them on fire. Use gasoline. Got that?"

Sikes swallowed hard, "You think, I mean, those State Police guys could become ... zombies?"

"Don't know, but be suspicious, and be careful."

"Ah, Birch, maybe you need to come out here? Take a look at ... "

"I gotta go, Herman. Handle it, please!" Ellroy hated to cut the call but he had another call he needed to take right away from Doctor Carter. "Yeah, doc, sorry, I was on the line with Herman. What's up?"

"Look, I got a situation here. Jake and his two sons came in, the boys are bit bad, by the members of the Carmody Family. I fixed the boys up, but I didn't want to tell Jake his sons might be infected. Both are running a fever now and they don't respond well."

"You think the bites they got from those things might kill 'em?"

"I can't say, Birch, but they're not getting better."

"And if they die from those bites ... ?"

"That's it, you gotta get here and talk to Jake, convince him of what we might have to do if things get to ... you know? If things get to that point."

"All right, dammit! Look, you be careful, doc, watch them two boys like a hawk, they could turn any moment."

"You don't have to tell me that, Birch."

"Yeah, guess not, after what you've seen. By the way, did Jake and his sons bring in the Carmody Family bodies? They'll need to be burned."

"Don't know, didn't see them in the truck. I'll ask Jake."

There was a long momentary wait, then Jake Burlingame got on the phone.

"Birch, that you?"

"Yeah, Jake. What happened out there?"

"Them damn Carmody's is what happened. We found the corpses of the ma, pa and their daughter. They were dead, deader than dead, I tell you. Then they damn well came back to life and attacked my boys. I shot the things dead again. Sons of bitches hurt my boys, lit into them like hungry buzz saws. The damnedest thing I ever seen. I had to put them down again. I left them dead in the street in front of their house then set out to the doc's to get help for my boys. I shot them things each twice in the head, Birch, like you said, so I reckon they're done for. Not to worry."

Sheriff Birch Ellroy froze and looked around him carefully once again, but he knew he hadn't missed them. The Carmody's were nowhere to be seen.

"Birch?"

Ellroy realized this situation was getting out of control too fast and he had to fight to hold down his own panic. Four men dead and burned, then the Carmody's, now Jake's two sons — and the LaRontue Brothers were also still out there somewhere. God knows what they were doing! Then the State Police. He wondered what had happened to them.

"Birch, you there?"

"I'm out by the Carmody house now, Jake. There's no bodies anywhere around here at all."

"Oh." The word from the other end of the line was a nervous peep.

There was silence, then Doctor Carter got back on the line, in a lower and more careful voice. "Birch, I'm worried about Jake's sons. He's in the other room with them now. I think I might need your help here soon."

Ellroy sighed deeply. "Yeah, I guess so. I'll be right over."

The Sheriff closed his phone, pocketed it, and then suddenly had that creepy feeling come over him again, followed by the smell of death and decay that was up wind of him. He quickly drew his .45 and turned to see all three members of the Carmody Family; mother, father and the formerly lovely young Alice, coming towards him in a mad head-long rush of insatiable hunger and bestial fury. The family he had known, the good loving parents and the lovely young daughter of but days before had been turned into ghastly creatures of decay and rotting foul-smelling flesh. They came at him like insane things, mindless and non-human with a wild preternatural appetite for living flesh.

His flesh!

Sheriff Elroy held his fear in check and pushed back the bile rising from his throat. He released the safety on his .45 and took careful aim. Then he emptied the clip into each member of the Carmody Family, sending them sprawling back and downward by the impact of the slugs. He quickly re-loaded and emptied another clip into the head of each creature—he could not think of them as being human any longer. All three lay apparently dead in the street.

Ellroy wiped the sweat dripping from his face, allowed himself to take a deep breath. Thank God he had been able to drop all three of the hideous creatures before they had been able to reach him. He didn't know what he would do if he was ever bitten by one of these things—like Jake's boys had been. Even a scratch might prove fatal, or worse yet, he might become one of those damn things. How would he handle that if it happened, and what would it mean? He thought of his wife and son, then he prayed that he and his family would be protected and come through this safe and sound. He had considerable doubts.

Ellroy looked at the vile mass of decayed dead matter before him on the street. Once, these had been good people. Now they were just some kind of flesh-eating monsters.

They had become God-damned zombies!

He thanked the Lord that he had more cans of gasoline back in his Jeep. He retrieved one and quickly doused the pile of three bodies and then set them ablaze. The stench of burning flesh and rotting corpses assailed his nostrils. He wanted to look away, but his job dictated otherwise. He watched carefully as the fire consumed each of the three corpses, burning brightly and furiously on the dry husks of the dead creatures until all that was left was a small pile of ashes. This he scattered into the surrounding dirt and grass at the edge of the street with the toe of his boot so even the ashes did not remain together.

Chapter 16: Resistance

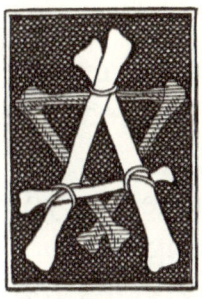N HOUR HAD PASSED and Sheriff Ellroy knew he had to be getting back to the doc's, but first he made a call to Trudy Nelson at the high school to update her.

"Birch, you okay? You don't sound so good," Trudy asked, curious with concern.

"I'm okay. I found the Carmodys."

"Oh, good, can you bring them in?"

There was silence for a moment until he figured out best how to say it.

"They won't be coming in," Ellroy stated flatly. "Look, Trudy, you still have some teams going out and picking up folks?"

"Yeah, Jake and his sons, and I got Simon Rees and Cathy Turner heading up teams to bring in more people."

"Forget about Jake and his sons for now. Alert your other teams to be watchful for the LaRontue brothers—and for any others of these things—these zombies or whatever they are. This sickness, or whatever it is, seems to be spreading and we need to get a handle on it before it gets out of control. Be suspicious of anyone who has bite marks or scratches, and of any corpses your people come across."

"I see, Birch, so it's that bad out there."

"You have no idea," he replied firmly.

"You okay?"

"Yeah, I'm just fine and dandy."

"Will we be getting any help from the state on this?" she asked hopefully.

"Yeah, but I have to get an update from Herman, there might be a problem with that. Look, Trudy, just have your people be extra careful out there. They're all armed, right?"

"Yes, pistols, hunting rifles, some shotguns, everyone is toting around here these days, makes me amazed they haven't all shot each other by mistake."

"Well, make sure everyone is armed and make sure you set some armed guards at each door of the high school. And board up the doors and windows, any vents too. Also, send out armed teams to gather food and water, and also cans of gasoline. We'll need all that—especially all the gas you can get."

"So it's that serious?"

"Yeah, it's that serious, Trudy. Also get the word out that the two LaRontue brothers are still loose. I think they are the source of all this but I have no idea how many others they may have infected. At some point they're going to run out of fresh meat with the last of the stragglers in the village. That means they're going to hit the outer farms, or more probably come into the village for your people at the high school."

Trudy Nelson shivered. Until this moment she'd just been reporting on the terror, helping out here and there as best she could, now it was all coming home to her in no uncertain terms that she'd soon be in a central part of it—or a potential victim. She was now thrust right into the center of the terror. She swallowed hard, nervous but determined.

"I understand you, Birch. How soon will you be here and will you bring Doc Carter? We got people in need."

"Anyone bitten?" he asked sharply.

"No, mostly the old that need medicine, one of the kids broke a finger, nothing serious, yet here ... but ... "

"But?"

"Mary Kent who runs the village Post Office hasn't been seen in a while. When Cathy Gamage came in here she told me she went to mail a letter this morning and Mary jumped out at her from ambush behind the counter; attacked her like some rabid beast. Mary's 75 years old, Birch, but Cathy said the old gal moved like some wild animal and she seemed real hungry. Cathy got out of there fast, but no one has seen Mary Kent and I'm worried about her."

"Okay, I'll keep a lookout for her and you do the same. Give me a few hours. I need to find out some things first, get them cleared up. Listen, tell your people if they come across any of those zombies, shoot them in the head. Then when they go down hurry up and pour gasoline on the bodies and set them on fire. It's the only way I know to stop them for good," Ellroy said and closed his phone before Trudy could ask more questions. He took one last look at the smudge of dark ashes on the center of the ground which was all that was left of where he'd set fire to the Carmody Family.

"Three down, how many more to go?"

He got into his Jeep and started driving.

"Herman? Herman, you there?"

Deputy Herman Sikes came back to reality after what he'd just been forced to look upon. He answered his phone with trepidation as if in a trance.

"Yeah, Birch, I'm here. I came out to the Spring Bridge like you asked. The place looks like the fire burnt out everything. A lot of dry weeds and grass here, the place must have went up like a tinderbox."

"Are you by the cars? Can you see them?"

"Yeah, and they're both State Police vehicles. I'm walking closer now. Everything is burned, I can barely make out the insignia on the cars but they're State Police for sure. There's bodies inside, four to a car. Damn!"

"What?"

"They're burned to a crisp!"

"You sure? All of them are dead?" Birch asked, knowing the worst had to be true.

"They never had a chance, Birch. Both cars went over the rail headlong into the ravine and burst into flames. They were all cooked alive. Think they were drunk?"

"No, of course not. I want to ask you something, Herman, since you're there on the scene. You think they could have done this on purpose? Maybe something caused them to loose control? Or they went through the guardrail on purpose?" Ellroy asked his deputy.

"I don't see how. What makes you say that?"

"Tell me what Elmer said."

"Well, the old man witnessed the whole thing, he's a farmer out here. He told me it looked to him like the cars drove off the bridge on purpose. I just can't figure it though. He said it looked like one just followed the other. Now why do you suppose he said that?" Sikes asked curiously, for these were outsiders to the parish. There was no way any of them could have been infected by this zombie germ unless they'd met up with one of the things on the road into the parish. He told this theory to Ellroy.

Ellroy didn't respond, instead he asked, "So everything's really well burned as far as you can see. Especially the bodies."

"Oh, yeah, burned to a crisp, I think. The bodies look to be almost dried out ash."

"Almost?" Ellroy asked carefully.

"Well, yeah, pretty much I think," Sikes replied.

"All right, Herman, leave it be for now. Pick up that old man, Elmer, but check him out carefully. Make sure he's got no bite marks or scratches on him. If he does, call me back right away. If he's clean run him over to the high school and hand him over to Trudy Nelson. Then meet me at Doc Carters. Got it?"

"Sure, Birch, but … "

"But what?"

"You think these were the State Police and FBI boys that were sent out to help us?"

"It appears so," Ellroy replied grimly.

"So then we won't be getting any help on this?"

"It appears so," Ellroy repeated, then he cut the connection and headed to Doc Carter's office.

As Sheriff Ellroy drove up to the medical building he spotted Doctor Carter standing at the front railing having a cigarette.

Ellroy got out of his Jeep and walked on over. The headache of the day before was beginning to reassert itself, like a nagging companion that he just couldn't drop.

"Hey, Howie," Ellroy said with a forced grin, "still with the cancer sticks, I see."

"Hey, Birch," Carter said between puffs. "I can't stop smoking now. No way! I think we're going to have our hands full with Jake. One of his sons just died, the other seems on the way. High fever. I gave him the best medicine I have to bring the fever down as well as antibiotics to fight any infection. I even tried an ice bath, nothing seems to work on bringing down the fever. Without knowing exactly what this is, I don't really know how to treat it."

"Well, I know you're doing the best you can. Did you check their blood?"

"Yes, I ran all the standard tests, and some not so standard ones. It's nothing I've ever seen before. If it is some kind of virus or bacteria, I've never run across it," the doctor replied. "Right now I'm concerned about how Jake will take this... I mean, he's angry and hurt but I don't think his mind has connected yet with the reality of what must be done."

"Yeah, like that his sons will come alive again and attack him. I don't think he's gonna cotton to us setting them on fire either, and we must do that before they reanimate," Ellroy stated. "Where are they?"

"Lying on tables in the room in the back."

Ellroy checked his .45, took off the safety. "Okay, let's go."

Doctor Carter led Sheriff Ellroy into the back surgery room where they saw old Jake Burlingame standing between two tables upon which his sons Burl and Barney lay. One of the boys was already dead. Ellroy thought it was Burl, or maybe it was Barney; he could never tell them boys apart.

Jake's back was towards the dead son as he tried to administer a drink through the parched lips of the still living son. That boy had a high fever, looked bland and seemed to be growing gray and leaning into death even as they watched. Jake was crying, whispering softly to his remaining son, begging him not to die. It was tragic to see. He hardly noticed that Ellroy and the doctor had entered the room.

Sheriff Ellroy holstered his gun and watched the terrible scene played out before him with great sadness. First the Carmodys and now Jake's two sons. But the sheriff knew what had to be done. It wouldn't be pleasant. Knowing Jake, it might even prove dangerous. Ellroy just wasn't sure how he was going to manage it.

First thing Ellroy did was gingerly pick up Jake's shotgun from where it was leaning against the wall and hand it to the doc standing behind him. He motioned for Carter to place the weapon outside the room, so it couldn't be brought into action if there was any trouble from Jake.

Then the sheriff walked over toward Jake Burlingame. The big man was lovingly closing the eyes of his second and last son, who had just passed away. It was a tough break.

"I'm sorry, Jake," Ellroy told him.

"Why?" Jake asked, looking back and forth at his two dead sons in utter disbelief and shock. Anger had not set in yet, but it surely would soon.

"Jake? Are you all right?"

"All right? What the hell do you think, Sheriff!"

"I know, I understand ... but we have to take them now."

"Wait one minute. How the hell you know what I feel? How the hell you understand? You didn't loose no sons. Far as I know your Tommy is still alive and safe. Both my boys are gone now. They ain't going nowhere!"

Ellroy took a step back, he wasn't sure how to handle this and was afraid he had already messed it up.

Thankfully, Doctor Carter stepped up, put his hands on Jake's shoulders like a brother, then drawing close to him he whispered into the man's ear.

Jake was motionless and silent for a long time, but at least he was listening to what Carter was telling him. Carter kept talking to Jake real close, real low. Ellroy couldn't hear what was being said to the big man but it seemed to be having some effect.

"No!" Jake shouted suddenly.

"Yes!" Carter shouted back boldly, loudly. "And you know it! You know it, Jake! Think of your boys, and their mother. They'd never want that to happen to them. They're dead, they should stay dead. You're a God-fearing man, Jake. What's the *Bible* tell you about all this?"

Jake Burlingame was silent for a long moment, tears streaming down his face.

"Come on now, let me and Birch handle it. We'll do it proper, respectful," Carter promised.

Jake was silent for a moment, then looked at the doctor, "No, I want to be a part of it. They're my boys, my flesh and blood."

Doctor Carter looked at Sheriff Ellroy who nodded his assent.

"Okay, Jake, you can be a part of it but we have to wheel them outside now, before they come back ... Then place them out on the lawn and get the gasoline," Carter told him softly but in a firm tone. There was nothing else to do now.

Jake nodded glumly. He understood now what needed to be done.

They rolled the tables out of the room and down the hall. They let Jake carry each of his sons, one by one, out of the building where he carefully and lovingly placed each body down upon the green grass of the outside yard.

He placed the bodies of both boys next to each other. Then Doctor Carter brought over a five gallon can of gasoline. He'd had one of the neighbor boys stock up cans of gas for him at the local Exxon. The doctor placed the can in front of the dead bodies of the two boys and then stepped away. The father walked over, picked up the can and began to douse the bodies of his sons with the gasoline. It was a surreal event.

Ellroy noticed that this was being done none too soon, for he saw the bodies beginning to twist and twitch with the renewal of reanimated life.

"Hurry up, Jake," Doctor Carter warned. "They're coming back to life."

Jake Burlingame grew frantic with tears and pain but he upended the gas can and thoroughly doused the bodies of his sons, then he lit a match and set them ablaze.

It was a huge bonfire and the smell of roasting flesh and burning hair was appalling. Utterly horrific. The three men watched silently, each with his own grim thoughts. The father, now a shell of a man, had descended to a place beyond despair and beyond hopelessness even. The sheriff and the doctor were saddened by the tragic loss, but relieved that at least two more of the monsters were now put down forever.

The fire burned brightly and long. None of the three men said a word. After almost an hour, when the ashes were all that was left on a brown, singed spot of ground, Doctor Carter went over to the father of the boys and hugged him with tears, "God rest their souls."

Afterwards Sheriff Ellroy and Doctor Carter loaded up the doc's car with everything he might need at the high school. Jake helped, seeking to do something useful and keep his mind off what had just happened. Plenty of time for grief later on — if they were successful and they lived through this nightmare.

Chapter 17: The School

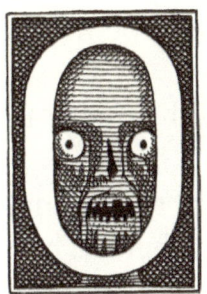**NCE** AT MACEDONIA CENTRAL HIGH SCHOOL, Sheriff Birch Ellroy immediately ran to find his wife Sue, and his boy, Tommy. He hugged them to him dearly, relieved to see them again. They looked none the worse for wear, but scared, like everyone else in the building—or as it had now become—the fortress of last refuge.

"You've done a good job here," Ellroy told Trudy Nelson when he and the doc met with her.

"I tried my best, Birch. Sue helped a lot. What about the State Police?"

Ellroy sighed. "They had an accident out by Spring Bridge. They're all dead. We won't be getting any help from them, or anyone else, for a while. We're on our own."

Trudy Nelson looked glum. "I don't know how long we can hold out here. Food and water's running low. I've been sending out teams to go into the markets and stores to pick up food and stuff we need as you told me to but... How long you figure this is going to last, Birch?"

"I don't know," Ellroy replied truthfully.

Trudy digested those words with a sigh. "Well, is it spreading? There's a lot of talk and there's a lot of people we've been unable to reach. Sue and I have also been phoning them but they don't answer. I send the teams out to collect them but more often than not lately they come back empty-handed. But they tell me they've seen some of these dead things out there — some they recognize — walking around. Zombies!"

"Any idea how many your people have seen?" Ellroy asked.

Trudy shook her head, "Dozens for sure, maybe more. A lot of people are missing, Birch."

Sheriff Ellroy nodded grimly. What could he say to that?

Doctor Carter weighed in. "I think it's safe to say that we have two for sure, the two LaRontue brothers. Then you have to assume that anyone we can't find or who hasn't come into the high school yet ... well, by now they could be one of them too. They may all be infected."

"My God, that's ... from my list, all the people that are missing ... that's over a hundred people!" Trudy said with growing concern. "You said infected? Is this some kind of disease? Is there an antidote or medicine for it?"

Doctor Carter sighed. "That's just my best guess about what is happening, Trudy. I haven't found anything conclusive on any infection yet. I don't see any particular virus or bacteria. I tried various medicines and antibiotics on Jake's boys but nothing worked."

"I heard about them," Trudy said sadly. "How's he taking it?"

"Badly," Ellroy said. "He's devastated. I'd feel the same way if it was my Tommy."

Trudy nodded then asked, "Did you really have to set fire to the corpses?"

"Yes, but Jake did it himself, he wanted to do it," Carter stepped in to explain. "That's the only way we know how to kill these things for good. Even if you shoot them — in the heart, in the brain — it doesn't matter, they will eventually reanimate. Cut them into pieces and the pieces will reanimate. Burning them seems to be the only remedy to kill them for good. So that they stay dead."

"Son of a bitch!" Trudy stammered.

"So now you know," Doctor Carter added. "Spread the word to the people here and to your recovery teams. They are to immediately burn any corpses they come across by dousing them completely with gasoline. Anyone actually bit or scratched by one of these creatures will probably come down with the disease also. We need to be proactive and find these people too. They will get sick, weak with a high fever, then die. Then they'll reanimate. Then they'll look for food. That will be us! We have to burn them, right after they die, before they reanimate."

Trudy Nelson just shook her head in disbelief and horror. "It's the end of the world."

"It's the end of Macedonia Parish if we don't tackle this problem and win. We can win. First thing we have to do is find those LaRontue brothers and put them down for good — forever," Carter said.

Sheriff Ellroy was thinking the exact same thing, but where would they find the creatures? They seemed to hide by day and go hunting in the dark of night. It was late afternoon now, so they'd be coming out soon, hunting for warm, living, human flesh. Ellroy thought about that, wondering where they could be hiding and then he had one of his hunches.

"You guys should be safe here for the time being," Ellroy told Trudy and the doc. "Keep your guards out all night, set them up in shifts, armed and ready."

"Where are you going, Birch?" Trudy and his wife, Sue, asked simultaneously.

"This whole thing started out by LaRontue Mansion in that damn grave when we pulled out the bodies of those brothers. Those things gotta be hiding out in the day. They gotta be staying somewhere. Why not in that house they grew up in? Or even in that grave? I also want to talk with that witch, Sabella, if I can find her. Maybe she knows something that could be helpful."

"That could be a long shot, Birch," Carter said with a perplexed look, "but you might be right. Maybe some vestiges of home or familiarity still reside in these creature's memory; they may see that house as a safe haven."

"That's what I'm thinking. Anyway it's a hunch and I gotta try something to find them. This is the best idea I have right now," Ellroy stated. He went to say goodbye to his wife and son, never letting on to her and his boy that it might be for the last time.

"Sue, I'm just going out on a run, to check something out. I should be back in a few hours."

"Do you have to go, Birch?" his wife asked, almost pleading, she'd seen so little of him the last few days. She was scared and wanted him around—she needed him around.

"Yeah, I'm sorry, but I have to go."

"Be careful, please."

"I will."

"Be careful, Daddy," young Tommy added. "You know how to kill the zombies. Make them all die for good."

"I'm trying to, son."

Birch Ellroy picked up his son, hugged his wife to him tightly. "Don't worry, I'll be back, then we'll clean up this mess and everything will be back to normal."

"I hope so, Birch," Sue told him softly, not believing a word of what he'd just told her. Normal was destroyed around here forever.

On the way out of the building Ellroy stopped by to see his deputy, Herman Sikes.

"Everything running smoothly here, Herman?"

"Sure, Birch, the last of the pick-up parties is back now. Getting late, it will be dark soon. Where you going? Heading out?"

"Yeah."

"That a good idea, boss? Where to?"

"Back to LaRontue Mansion," Ellroy told him. "I want you to keep everything calm here and help Trudy and Sue to get things organized."

"I will, you can count on me, Birch, but do you think it's wise to go out there now. It'll be dark soon," Sikes said, fearful for his boss but glad he'd not been asked to accompany him.

"Just something I gotta check out, Herman. I'll see you in the morning."

Once he left the school Ellroy stopped at the village police station and picked up four boxes of ammo. A few more guns. He also grabbed up a pump shotgun and a few boxes of shells. On the way out of the village he stopped by the Exxon station and re-filled his four five-gallon cans with gasoline. He left a note on the counter to Sammy Palmario who owned the station and was nowhere to be seen for what he owed. If Sammy was even still alive. Then Ellroy set out to LaRontue Mansion.

Chapter 18: The Hunch

 **HE** DRIVE OUT WAS LONG AND LONELY and his damn headache was coming back full force again. This time Sheriff Birch Ellroy hardly noticed it, nor cared. He had a swirling tornado of thoughts in his mind with so many unanswered questions. What *if* this? What *if* that? What was he going to do about all this? He had no idea. He knew that if he found anything out here—and that was a big *if* since this was just some lame-brained hunch he had—he'd have to play everything by ear and fit his actions to the circumstances. The darkness of the night that had never bothered him before, now seemed stifling and more fearful than it had ever been, full of lurking evil and horrible waiting doom.

"In other words," he said to himself grimly as he drove the empty highway, "I'm scared shit and I have no plan."

On the way out to the old mansion he came across some people. He stopped by the Weller farm. Cathy Weller and her four kids were all there. He found them safe and fit, told them there was an emergency and they needed to head into the village right away.

"Is it them damn terrorists?" Cathy Weller asked curious, an angry gleam in her deep blue eyes.

Ellroy allowed a slim smile. He only wished that it were, "No, but it is a real emergency, anyone alone out here is in danger. You've gotta leave right now and get you and the kids to the high school in the village right away."

He saw to it that they were all armed and watched them drive off in their truck. He wished them well and hoped they'd make it. Then he continued his drive.

He came across a car crashed into the highway guard rail a few miles further on. The vehicle had out of state plates. There was no body or bodies. That indicated the people might still be alive and had walked off to get help—or they could have been killed then walked away as zombies. He didn't know which it might be. He had no time to stop and look now.

He did stop a mile further on when he came upon an old man and woman lying by the side of the highway. Their throats had been torn out. It had been done recently. He knew they were newly dead and would soon reanimate. He watched with sickening revulsion as they slowly twitched and turned and struggled to come back to that evil bogus life the zombies showed. Ellroy very business-like put a bullet in each of their heads, then quickly doused them with gasoline and set them ablaze. He didn't linger to ensure the completeness of his handiwork but got back into his Jeep and sped off towards LaRontue Mansion.

It was a grim journey out this far into the corner of the parish. It was a rural, lonely bayou swampland, but he made it to the gate of the estate before full dark set in, and of that at least he was thankful. He drove down the tree-lined road and stopped in front of the huge and foreboding mansion in the oval driveway. He got out of the Jeep, taking the loaded shotgun with him.

"Come on, you bastards, show yourselves!" he growled under his breadth as he approached the house. He knew why he had come out here and what he wanted to do.

He quickly went around the building behind the house and over to the grave by the woods. This was the same patch of earth where he and Trudy Nelson had found the unmarked grave of the two LaRontue brothers bare days before. It seemed to Ellroy like all that had been ages ago now, so much had happened.

Warily, with the shotgun leveled and ready for action, he approached the open grave and looked down into it carefully.

"Dammit!" he growled in frustration and defeat. The grave was empty. It looked just as it had after the two bodies had been dug out of it days ago. It seemed untouched. The LaRontue brothers had never been back here. So where the hell could they be? Back in the village most likely — or perhaps, inside the house?

Ellroy couldn't know the answer to that question for certain but with his head throbbing and his gut churning nervously he knew what he had to do. It was that house. He had unfinished business there. He was out here now, after all. He might as well go inside the house and check it out. He knew he had to re-enter LaRontue Mansion and do a full room by room search. The prospect of that chilled him to the bone and gave him the creeps. But it had to be done. He knew he had to make sure the brothers were not hiding there.

Ellroy walked back around the building towards the front door. It was unlocked as it had been before and he slowly and carefully entered the mansion, the shotgun barrel pointed level and ready for business.

The place was quiet and seemed empty. That meant nothing. It was beginning to get dark so he wanted to put on the lights but the light switch didn't work. There was no electricity in the house now. No lights. He cursed the darkness, wondering vaguely why there was no electricity. Had Louisiana Light & Power turned it off already? It didn't matter. He knew he had to do his search regardless, checking each of the pitch-black rooms.

He decided to do this right and go back to his Jeep to get his flashlight when his cell suddenly buzzed. The sound shocked him and got his heart racing. Man, was he jumpy!

It was Trudy Nelson on the line.

"Yeah, Trudy?"

"Birch, you have to get back here right away. They're all outside! The zombies. Outside all around the school. They have us surrounded. We can see them by the streetlights, shambling around. They attacked one of my guards, Jose Ortiz. They just dragged him away screaming into the woods. I don't want to think about what they did to him. It was terrible." Trudy cried now, trying to hold down her hysteria. "We don't know what to do, Birch. They seem to be waiting until dark, then I think they're going to try to come inside and get us."

He knew what that meant.

"You have to hold out, Trudy. Make sure all the exits are locked and manned with armed guards. Did you see the LaRontue brothers there?" he asked.

"I don't know, I didn't, but Doctor Carter said he saw one of them — or something that looked like one of them. We're all terrified. Herman is near frantic, he's not a big help. We need you here."

"Okay, Trudy, I'm on my way. Are Sue and Tommy safe?"

"They're here with me, you want to talk to them?"

"Yeah, let me talk to Susan."

"Birch! What the hell's going on? They're out there now! Where did they all come from? There must be dozens of them," she cried, bravely trying to hold down her growing hysteria.

"Listen, honey, I'll be there soon. You and Tommy stay close to Trudy, Doc Carter and Herman. And you still have that .45 I gave you?"

"Yes," she stammered in between tearful sniffles.

"Good, then take the safety off like I showed you and keep it close and ready to use."

"I'm scared, Birch."

"I know, honey, I'll be there soon."

His search of the house for the brothers was moot now if they had been seen outside the high school. Ellroy closed his cell and got back into his Jeep and drove off leaving LaRontue Mansion behind him, he hoped forever.

Chapter 19: Back To School

HERIFF BIRCH ELLROY drove like a maniac down the highway through Macedonia Parish into the village and finally towards Central High School. The building and grounds were fairly lit up, but as he drove closer he slowed down his Jeep and became more careful, one hand on the steering wheel, the other on his .45. His eyes scanned the area around the school carefully. There were some local stores across the street, a track and field on the north side, and on the other side and in the back a piney woods that ran back at least five hundred yards.

He stopped the Jeep, took a better look before he went in closer. He wished he'd taken the night vision goggles from his office, but then realized that dead bodies gave off no heat signature, so they would be useless. He did his best to scan the area carefully, section by section.

Then he saw them. Ragged, gory, shambling figures, keeping to the shadows and the darkness, but they were there, like cockroaches. Vile, ugly things, of filth, decay, of the grave and death—and not-death. He silently scanned the area counting the things, and he came up with at least two dozen of them. The LaRontue brothers had been busy and they worked fast—the appetites of these creatures seemed insatiable. Now the high school containing all that remained of the helpless people of Macedonia Parish were within that makeshift fortress and under siege.

Sheriff Ellroy knew he had to get into that building and he had to make sure those zombies were unable to enter with him. He started up his Jeep and began to drive.

Suddenly he felt a loud and heavy thump to his vehicle. He was terrified to see one of the zombies land upon his hood trying to crawl up towards his windshield and get at him. Ellroy frantically drove in a sharp angular pattern to knock the damn thing off his vehicle but it hung on as if by magic. Finally Ellroy let loose with a few slugs from his .45 and the creature fell off the Jeep and he drove away. But then there was another thump, this time at his passenger side. Through the broken glass of the window another dead thing was now clawing for him with frantic, rabid hunger. Ellroy pointed his .45 at the thing's head ready to send it straight to hell, but the wily creature suddenly slapped the gun out of his hand. The .45 fell to the floor of the Jeep and the thing tried to drag itself through the window to get at Ellroy. It moaned and growled with a ravenous hunger that was terrible to hear and an appetite that was seemingly all-encompassing.

The Sheriff was frantic now, sweating bullets he grabbed up the shotgun from the passenger seat beside him and stuck the barrel into the mouth of the attacking creature and pulled the trigger. The blast shattered the zombie's head like a ripe melon, dead matter, pus and rot scattered out the window as what remained of the torso slid away down to the street.

"Goodbye, bastard!" the sheriff shouted as he sped away towards the high school.

By the time Ellroy reached the front of the school
building it had grown dark outside. He took out his cell
and called Trudy, telling her he was right outside at the
front entrance, and to be ready for him. He told her to
make sure that door was unlocked for him. Then he
drove right on up to the door, jumping out of his Jeep
like all the creatures of hell were after him. They were!
A dozen zombie-things were close upon him, closing
fast. Carrying his shotgun and his .45 he ran towards the
school door and was relieved when it suddenly opened
and his deputy, Herman Sikes, quickly pulled him inside
the building.

Deputy Sikes quickly shut the door and locked it behind
him with a chain and padlock. Ellroy clearly saw the
situation here and realized that while the zombies were
for the moment effectively locked out—the people were
also just as effectively locked in. The place could prove
a death trap. There'd be no escape for anyone as long as
those creatures were out there—and if those creatures
ever got into this building...

"Oh, Birch!" It was Susan, his wife, running over to
him now hugging him so tightly he could scarce believe
her strength—her fear. His son, Tommy, was with her
and hugged him too. They felt so good in his arms, a sight
for sore eyes, but he could feel their fear and it galled him
that he could not do anything to eliminate the danger they
were in.

Trudy Nelson and Doctor Carter were there now too. So
were some of the local people from the village. He could
see they were all traumatized by what had happened.

"You had a tight spot, Birch," Carter told him. "We
could see what happened as you drove up."

"Yeah, they attacked me. It was touch and go for a few moments," Ellroy admitted, sighing with nervous tension, as he looked at everyone around him, the faces, the hopeless faces. He saw the gymnasium had been set up as a relief center with cots. It must be housing a couple of thousand people, almost everyone from the village and the entire parish. At least he hoped so. It looked like Katrina all over again — Katrina with zombies. Everyone looked terrified. "I counted about two dozen of those things out there. They've surrounded the school and I'm sure they're going to attack here eventually. We have to make sure they don't get into the building. Is everyone armed, Herman?"

"We've passed out weapons to all the adults that want them, Birch, and most do, but how can we keep them things from getting into the building? There's a hundred windows, a dozen doors, crawlspaces."

"I'm concerned we've set ourselves up like trapped rats here, like those poor people in the Astrodome in New Orleans during Katrina. Trapped, with no way out!" Trudy told him fearfully.

"Look, we have to make the best of it. Fight them off, keep them out," Ellroy ordered. "They cannot be allowed to get in here. We'll make our stand here, in the gym. I see you've closed off all the doors, covered all the windows with plywood, placed armed guards. That's good. We must get through this night and I am sure that tomorrow will be better. The zombies are running out of people to hunt, I think their numbers will level off if we can keep them from any fresh meat. That means we must keep them out of here. Then we can hunt them down tomorrow in the daylight."

"You sound hopeful," Doctor Carter said carefully.

"We've got to get through tonight first. Now all of you, get to work. Get everyone into the gymnasium and make sure it is made into an impregnable fortress."

They worked all evening shoring up defenses, making sure every door and every window in the building—not just the gymnasium—was locked, secure, blocked off with wooden covers. Then guarded by armed guards. A few of the men and women used their dogs to stand guard with them. It was hoped the dogs might prove an early warning system in case of attack.

The rain began about that time. A hard driving downpour with loud thunder and flashing lightning that would be coming down all night. It just made everything more spooky, and everyone more nervous. The local villagers and the people of Macedonia Parish from some of the outlaying farms were all gathered together onto the floor of the gymnasium and huddled into one fearful, quivering mass of human misery.

"They've been pushed to the limit," Trudy Nelson noted of the people in the gym to the sheriff as he did a run down of the building with her, his deputy, and the doctor to check defenses.

Sheriff Ellroy noted that guards were posted at all doors, windows and other weak points—they were placed anywhere it was thought there was even the possibility of one of them things getting into the building. That was good. Trudy had done well.

"I can see that, Trudy," Ellroy said with determination. These were his people and he was going to protect them or die trying.

However, the things from outside had already tried to get into the high school. Shambling across the lawn to attack at the front of the building, or across the sports field in the back, banging relentlessly on the doors or windows seeking to break inside, they had tried to pry open those doors and windows to get at the fresh living flesh which they craved.

Thank God the damn reanimated things did not have the intelligence of the living, but they did seem to possess superhuman strength.

Shots were fired through the upstairs windows.

Some of the creatures were hit.

Lisa Bouly shouted out defiantly, "I hit one! I took him down. See! Look!"

She had, and the others at that guard station with her gave her a victorious round of shouts and high-fives—until moments later when they all saw the creature begin to move on the ground. It was slowly coming back to life, the corpse re-animating itself, even as they watched. Soon it stood up on its feet and shambled off.

"Damn!" someone growled watching the dead thing move away.

Lisa shot at it again, as did the other men and women there with her, but the thing walked off oblivious to their bullets on its endless hunt for fresh flesh.

"They're testing our defenses," Doctor Carter said.

Sheriff Ellroy nodded. If that was true, it was going to be a long night and the creatures would keep at it until they found some way to get inside. The thought was chilling and he didn't want to share the depth of his concern with those around him. He had to remain positive, and even hopeful to these people—his people—who were counting on him.

Ellroy did another check of the outer guard posts. The rain kept pounding the building relentlessly, blasting against the windows, pelting the roof, coming down in torrents. Ellroy looked outside and saw everything was obscured by total darkness of night now, and by the rain and wind. The few streetlights in the area offered little in the way of visibility. In a lightning flash he saw rain was now flooding the area. Only in occasional brief flashes of bright lightning could Ellroy even see the area around the school, an area already flooded, but he could just make out some of the shambling creatures in the dark roaming around near the building seeking an entrance.

"They're still out there, trying to find a way in," Ellroy told the guards at each station as he tried to shore up their spirits like a general before a battle. "So be watchful."

The sudden scream was bloodcurdling.

The sound loudly traveled the entire length and breadth of the building. It was from a terrified woman.

It was coming from inside the school!

"Where's that coming from?" Ellroy demanded in shock.

"Over there!" Trudy Nelson pointed and she ran to a far corner of the building. "It's from the woman's bathroom!"

"Damn! They're inside!" Ellroy shouted, drawing his .45 as he ran towards the bathroom. He flung open the door and flew inside, then stopped in his tracks by what he saw there. He was followed inside by Trudy, the doc, and his deputy. All four stood frozen at what they saw.

"Herman, I thought you had all the windows blocked and armed men placed on guard at all these weak points."

"Women complained about their privacy, Birch."

"Privacy? Too damn bad!" he growled, then he looked upon an image he'd never thought to see before—even with all the hellish things he'd seen the last few days.

There before him was a terrified teenage girl, Tom Stafford's daughter, Anna. She was a student at the high school. Anna stood in rigid shock, her back flush against the wall, mesmerized as she watched one of the dead things crawling though the broken glass of the small bathroom window.

It was a tiny window used only for ventilation, none of the things could ever get through it, none of the adult things that is. However this was a smaller zombie. It was stuck halfway through the window frame. With some extra effort it might just slip through. Everyone looked at it in horror as it tried to wriggle its small body through the window to get inside. It growled at the people in furious hungry rage.

It was just a child.

A child zombie.

Ellroy looked at the thing in utter disgust and shock. It was a child, no more than five years old. Ellroy muttered a silent prayer, then leveled his .45 and took aim, then a new horror struck him when he realized he recognized the thing.

It was little Willy! The son of one of his neighbors, and a playmate of his son, Tommy.

"Jesus, it's little Willy Simon!" Ellroy said in anger, then he shook his head sadly and pulled the trigger. The thing was hit and squirmed in the window frame, screamed in rage, then Ellroy shot again and it shuddered and died.

For now.

Trudy Nelson took the terrified teenage girl out of the restroom after Doctor Carter checked her for bites or scratches. She was untouched. Then they escorted her to her father over in the gym.

There was utter chaos and fearful rumors for a long while that the sheriff and his deputy had to tamp down. The people were on a frantic knifepoint edge, but the zombies had not gotten into the school. Not yet.

"What now, Birch?" his deputy asked with a shiver. "One almost got in here. They will try again and next time one might get in."

"I know," Ellroy answered his deputy, examining the bathroom. The place seemed sturdy, safe, but...they'd almost got in once. "Herman, I want this bathroom closed off. Lock the door, board it up tight. And set a guard here outside. Got it?"

"Got it," his deputy said and set off to work.

"And Herman, get someone to get that thing out of the window, and burn it!"

Herman Sikes nodded. "I'll get Jake Burlingame, he'll set it ablaze."

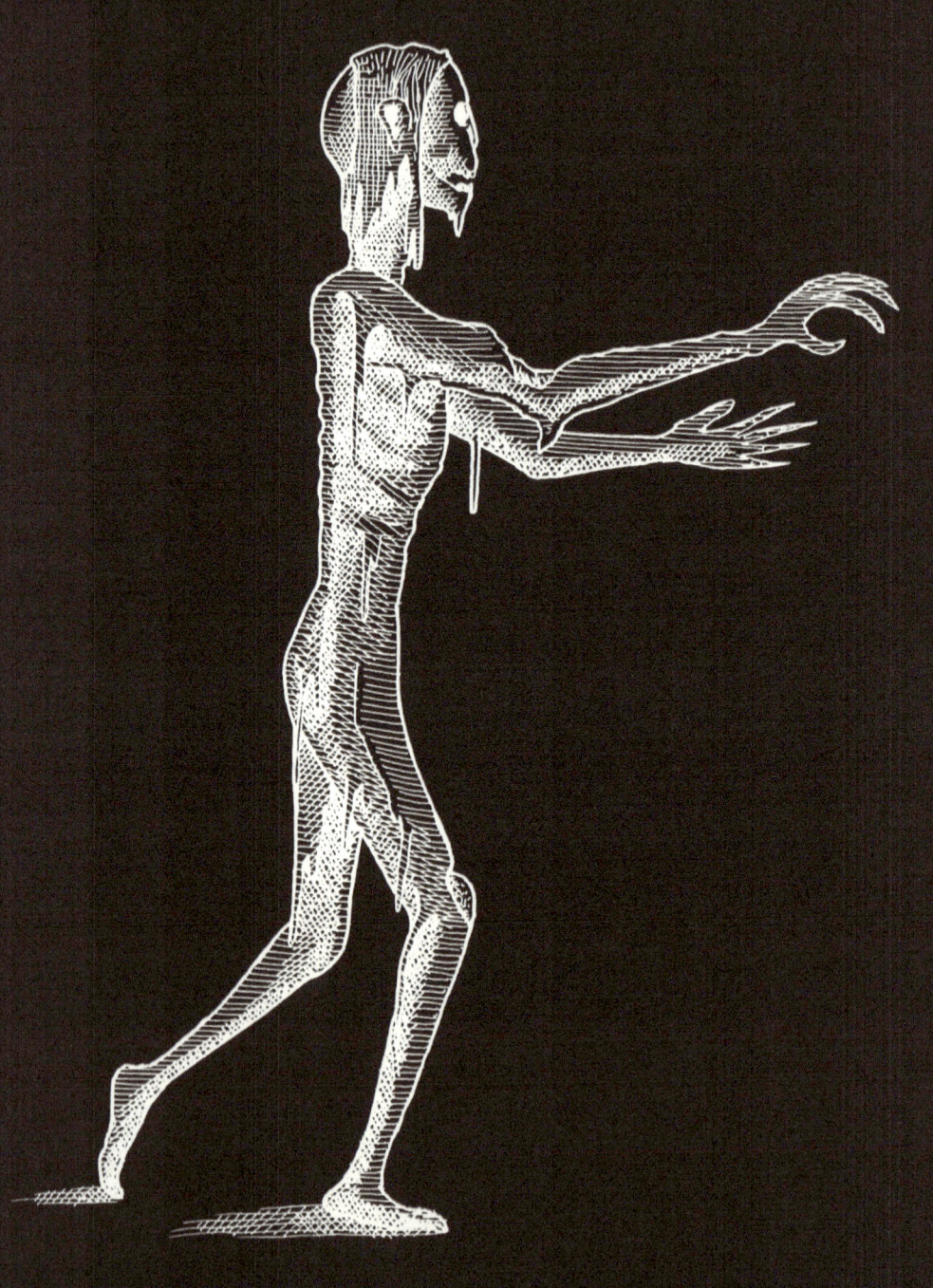

Chapter 20: Breakthrough

**UTSIDE** THE BATHROOM in the gymnasium, Ellroy held an impromptu meeting with Trudy and Doctor Carter who had now returned. Aside from the continual pelting rain on the roof and against the windows, and the loud thunder, they also heard from time to time sounds from the zombies testing their security. The things were trying to break into the building anywhere they could find a weak spot. Ellroy realized there could be many weak spots for them to enter. It was eerie. The creatures were continually banging upon the doors, their thin dead fingers constantly seeking to find any opening no matter how small, or any manner of entrance.

"Persistent bastards!" Doc Carter allowed grimly.

"They're hungry," Trudy explained, with a grim look, shuddering.

"We're doomed!" someone in the gym suddenly shouted.

Ellroy looked out to see a woman standing up in horror as her husband jumped up to embrace her, trying to quiet her down. Her fear had scared some of the younger children but the sheriff was glad to see the woman had quieted herself for the moment. More outbursts like that and the fragile hold they had over their fear would break down into chaos, and eventually doom and death.

"I don't like it, Birch. We're under siege here. The people are terrified, near panic," Trudy warned, holding down her own panic as best she could. She didn't even want to think of what she would do if one of those things came for her — or one of the children.

"I know," Ellroy replied, realizing that if a panic began no one would be able to control these people and they'd be open game for a zombie feast. He had to think. Something was wrong here, something didn't seem right to him now.

It came to him in a flash. He realized the things outside had suddenly become very quiet. Was that because the rain and thunder had become so loud it drowned out their incessant noise? Or was it something else? Something worse?

"Look," Ellroy said quickly to Trudy and the others, "we have to anticipate how these things will get into the building. Some of them *will* get in. I know you don't want to hear that but I'm afraid that's the reality. They have all night to try us, so it's just a matter of time before they find a way in, somehow. We need to anticipate their moves, think outside the box so we can be ready for them."

Ellroy admitted that the doc had been right about the bastards being persistent. Their hunger for living flesh seemed insatiable. He thought of the roof, the basement, crawlspaces, the air conditioning ducts, the windows on the second floor. There were just too many possibilities and he didn't have enough armed people to secure them all. He suddenly froze with fear, looking with alarm at Trudy.

"The basement? Are there windows down there?"

Trudy Nelson looked at Ellroy a bit startled, then

sudden shock came to her face. "I'm not sure. I never thought of it. I mean, I don't remember any, but … "

Doctor Carter chimed in alarm, "I think there might be, Birch. One small window on each side, but very small windows, if I remember correctly. Much too small for an adult body to get through—but a child could get through it. But something else just came to me. There's also a coal chute in the back of the building from the old days that has never been cemented shut. If they can open that, we're in real trouble."

Ellroy nodded. It worried him that the zombies had been quiet for a while, so he knew they had to be up to something.

It was too late now and too dangerous to send a team down into the basement to muck around there and close any open windows or check out the coal chute. Who knew what they'd find there now? Sending anyone down there would be a death sentence for them. For now it looked like that old coal chute had been left untouched by the creatures, or they just hadn't found it yet. What couldn't be ignored was the nagging thought in the sheriff's mind that the zombies had already found some way into the basement and were even now trying to get up into the upper floor where all the people were.

Ellroy called out for his deputy, Herman Sikes, "Get me a dozen people with guns and meet me at the lower level of the central steps."

"Where the basement door is?" Sikes asked nervously.

"Yes, and hurry!"

Sikes went off on his mission. Ellroy, Trudy and the doc—the last two now carrying pump shotguns courtesy of the Macedonia Parish Sheriff's Department—began a frantic run to the center of the huge building.

The trio ran down the large and ornate granite central stairway to the lower landing. There they saw an enormous metal door and a tall black man on guard in front of it. He was carrying a .22 bird rifle, of all things.

"Sheriff Ellroy, damn glad you're here now." Mychal Elkins said nervously. The big man was scared but he was brave to keep his post here all alone. "I sent Quan looking for you. They're down there, I can hear 'em movin' around. Lots of 'em!"

Ellroy could hear the creatures too. They were definitely inside the building! An icy chill seized him. He could hear them shambling around in the huge basement down below. They were searching for a way to get upstairs. They were pounding on the walls, the door, desperately seeking any way up and inside.

Trudy Nelson blanched in terror. Doctor Carter stepped back nervously, lowered his shotgun level and waiting in case the damn things suddenly broke through the door. It was tense, the creatures continued to pound on the door, harder, louder, heavier, and for a moment it appeared they might break through.

"See what I'm talking about?" Elkins said, his eyes looking at that weakening door.

The door was metal, a fire door, set in a stout metal frame, but it was old and being pounded and pushed from inside relentlessly. It was not made to take this kind of punishment. The sheriff could see that it was buckling slightly.

Would it hold?

At that point it was anyone's guess.

Deputy Sikes arrived with a dozen men, all packing shotguns and automatic rifles. Young Jeff Quan was also with them, the Vietnamese fellow who had been on guard here with Mychal Elkins.

The men took up positions, more than a dozen weapons of various types aimed at the door, ready for what might come through that portal at any moment—should it burst open.

"That door won't hold," one of the men stated coldly.

"Look, it's buckling already," another man added, his voice full of fear.

The pounding was fierce now, growing stronger, Ellroy feared the preternatural strength possessed by the undead could burst the door open any moment.

Then suddenly the pounding stopped.

There was dead silence.

Everyone looked at everyone else with a mixture of alarm, relief, curiosity. What now?

Mychal Elkins put down his .22 rifle and went up close to the door. He put his ear up against the cold metal, motioning for everyone to be quiet.

There was a long moment of nervous tension and doubt in the total silence.

"I think...they're gone," Elkins stated curiously. "Wait, I can hear them on the other side, they seem to be trudging off."

"Off?" someone asked, not knowing if she felt alarm or relief.

"Yeah, they're moving off, but where are they going?" Trudy Nelson added ominously.

"Where is a good question," Deputy Sikes stammered in fear.

That was *the* question.

The men and women there at the bottom of the stairwell

looked around them, up and down, right and left, as if the zombies might magically appear out of the cement block walls all around them. No one had an answer as to where the things had gone. Some hoped they had just given up and gone away, but no one with any hold on reality left could really believe that. Then their eyes looked over to Sheriff Birch Ellroy, expectantly. They began to talk among themselves. Fear talk, growing near panic as Trudy and Doc Carter tried to keep things calm.

"We'll get them," Doc said, talking tough. "They can't get in here, right Trudy?"

Trudy nodded unconvincingly, then remembered she had to put up a bold front and said in a firmer voice, "Sure, they won't get in, all we have to do is keep watch."

Ellroy said nothing. He had no quick answer for what had happened, no understanding for it, but he tried to think it through. What was the best course of action now? Obviously the things had found a way into the building. But where? Where were they going? Where were they now? The sheriff knew that these things wanted to eat the human flesh of the living people huddled upstairs in the gym. That was the key, so that had to be their ultimate destination.

"Mychal, you and Quan stay here. Let me know if they make another try to get through this door. And Mychal?"

"Yeah, Sheriff Ellroy?"

"Get a bigger gun, please," Ellroy pleaded with a grin, then with more force he spoke to the others around him. "The rest of you come with me. I think they're into the air-conditioning ducts. They're trying to find some way to get at the people in the gym upstairs."

Chapter 21: Zombie Attack

HERE WERE CRIES OF ANGER AND FEAR now at the news. Most of the people had family in the gym, and had thought they were safe there. Until now. This news alarmed them and shook their resolve.

Ellroy wasn't so sure about his theory, but he remembered seeing those AC ducts in the gym, large aluminum box-like tunnels set overhead for the air to flow. They were the old style ones, set up high but there were also some wall ducts that were even bigger, low down by the floor, almost like doorways into the gym. Of course, they all had metal vents or screens on them, but they were old, some of them were rusted. He had had all of them covered with boards and bolted shut—but a sudden fear shook him now. Had they secured them all? Had one of them been missed? It only took one weak point to doom them all now.

The shocking answer came to him as he was leading his group up the central stairway. He heard terrified cries and screams coming from the gymnasium. People were in the throes of absolute panic and hysterical terror.

"Come on!" Ellroy shouted, and he and his group ran towards the sound of the screams.

There the sheriff saw a mob of terrified people huddling in one corner of the huge gym as a dozen men and women fought hand to hand with a group of zombies that had gotten into the gym from a far wall. Ellroy could see instantly how the things had gotten inside. The AC duct behind the piano had not been boarded up. Worse yet, there appeared to be no grill on the duct so the creatures had just moved the piano away that had blocked the wall for probably 20 years, and then swarmed into the gym. They were on the people before anyone knew what had happened.

The battle was fast and furious but most people fled in terror. Many men and women—fathers and mothers all—took their children and left. Others stood firm, shooting the invading things, using clubs and bats, doing anything to protect their families. The zombies went down one by one but it seemed another one just took their place and they just kept coming into the gym through that opening. There seemed to be an endless amount of them too. What made the event even more horrific was that most of the living there now recognized the dead—those reanimated dead were neighbors, friends, and some were even members of their own families.

Sheriff Ellroy and his team got there just in time and immediately started shooting down the invaders. Rounds of ammo from dozens of types of weapons shot into the shambling zombie horde that seemed to be on a relentless attack. Now that they had found a way into the school building, into the gym where the warm living flesh they craved was located, they would not let anything stop them. Even bullets. The dead things had to be shot down multiple times before they would stay down—but only for a few minutes—then they reanimated once again. For these living dead, even death itself was merely temporary.

Ellroy ordered his people in a stark shouting voice, "Spread out! Make a defensive wall here so none of them can get through us!"

His orders were followed quickly by anyone with a weapon and the cordon he set up protected the women and children for the moment, putting a wall of armed defenders between them and the relentless zombie attackers.

The dead things continued frantically forward, first by the tens, then by the dozens, young and old, male and female, teenagers and children. All were furiously hungry. Ellroy and his companions recognized many of the creatures now, he knew most of them as friends and neighbors. Or, once they had been, but now…

One woman behind the shooters recognized her own daughter who had gone missing. She screamed the child's name, then broke through the defensive line and ran towards her daughter, crying for her lost child. "Maria! It's Mommy! Don't be scared! Mommy's here!"

The daughter, now no longer the sweet child she had once been, having since transformed into a dead zombie thing, shambled quickly towards the running woman who embraced her daughter lovingly.

"Oh, Maria! Maria! Mommy's here!"

The Maria-thing subsequently grabbed the mother in a death grip and buried its mouth into the woman's neck, ripping her jugular and then began feasting on an orgy of warm, wet blood. It growled hungrily. Other zombies joined in the feast. It was horrific and had been so sudden. For a brief second everyone watched in shock and disbelief, then a dozen guns fired into the thing that had once been Maria, cutting it into pieces. It fell down seemingly dead—for now. For a short while—but everyone there knew it would be back alive soon.

"There's dozens of these things here," Ellroy shouted in the noise and confusion to Trudy Nelson who was now at his side. "How many people do you have listed as missing?"

"A hundred at least," Trudy shouted back.

"A hundred!" Ellroy stammered, shocked by the large number of people—his people—affected by this horror. Then he was struck by another thought. Any of the people these zombie-things had just attacked and bitten were also now potential candidates to join the ranks of the undead. Some lay on the floor dead or dying, others wounded and bleeding out from the initial attack or being feasted upon by more of the undead things as they entered the gymnasium ravenous with blood-lust. Some of the defenders had received just a tiny scratch—which would transform into a death sentence and worse for them very soon. The zombie ranks had not stabilized, they were still growing!

Ellroy saw to it that a steady stream of gunfire was kept up against the attacking things and it was working, but his people had to reluctantly move back. They had to create an ever-widening arc as the things relentlessly poured into the gym and tried to overwhelm the defenders by sheer numbers.

"Where are they all coming from?" Ellroy said, noting the seemingly never-ending flow of the undead into the gym. "How many of these things are there?"

The zombies seemed unstoppable, a wave of deathless dead, forever shambling forward in search of warm human flesh and blood. They were ravenous. Insatiable. Maybe even unstoppable.

"Move back! Keep firing!" Ellroy barked his orders to the defenders. Then to his deputy, "Herman, round up everyone with a gun, get everyone from all the other posts and bring them here right away."

"You think that's wise, Birch? You'll be stripping the other guard posts."

"It doesn't matter now, the things are already here, we need more firepower if we're going to stop them."

"Okay, right away," then Deputy Sikes was off.

Mychal Elkins and Quan See-Lo filled in Sikes position in the shooting line once the deputy had gone.

"Thought we'd come up and give a hand," Elkins told the sheriff. He showed Ellroy he had, in fact, got a bigger gun. It was a large caliber hunting rifle.

"Welcome to the party," Ellroy gave the big man a grim smile as they all continued pumping lead into the group of advancing undead monsters relentlessly coming towards them.

The battle raged with relentless destruction from both sides. The zombies would not stop, would not so much as slow down, they were inhuman eating machines seeking warm living flesh and blood. They seemed maddened by the very smell of the living. Meanwhile, the living were appalled by the horror of these dead things coming for them and their family, the bloody mess, the terrible odor, the frenzied insane bloodlust in their soulless eyes. Then on those times when they were able to pull down a living defender—their devouring feasting began. It continued until the things were shot to pieces, blown apart by the dozens of slugs from the terrified people still alive and pumping hot lead into them.

Ellroy noted that many of the creatures he had seen hit, and that had gone down apparently dead at the beginning of the attack, were now moving and twitching, seeking to reanimate themselves even as he watched. They were getting set to resume their attack, their endless quest for human flesh. Ellroy watched in amazement. They were now standing up, or crawling forward, in non-stop attack mode.

"I kilt that one before already!" Joe Clement shouted in frustrated anger. "Now he's up and coming at me again! That ain't right! Stay dead, damn you!"

"I killed this one twice already!" Tabor Evans shouted back to his friend and neighbor. "Now he's back at me for a third time and I'm sure gonna give it to him!"

The shooting, the smoke, the loudness of hundreds of reports reverberating throughout the huge gymnasium made it a bloody mad house. It was all made worse by the echo in the place. It caused the gym to reverberate with horrible eat-piercing hammering sounds. The terror was palpable. The mob of almost two thousand people packed behind the defensive line of gunmen had become a quivering mass of terrified humanity fearing the advancing zombies would break through that thin line at any moment and then begin their feast upon them.

Some of the people ran off, fleeing into other areas of the building to hide in shivering terror, others even made the decision to run outside the building, preferring to take their chances out in the open. That was a fatal mistake, Ellroy knew, but he had no time for them now. They'd have to take their chances. They'd made their choice and it was their death sentence.

The sheriff and everyone with him were in a battle for their very lives with a huge new mass of shambling undead things. This group had just burst into the gym. The defenders were grimly fearful, but they continued to shoot, re-load, and shoot again. Like automatons they mechanically did the grim work of shooting and killing. Even as the things they killed came back to life to attack them once more minutes later.

"I need more ammo!" a man in the line up ahead shouted. "Anyone got any double ought shot?"

"Anyone got any extra .38 slugs?" a woman barked frantically.

"I need .45 rounds! I'm down to just one clip!" someone else screamed nervously.

"Make your ammo count! Don't waste your shots!" Ellroy barked out the order. He figured his people had joined this fight with enough ammo for a war, but it had not been enough. They desperately needed more ammunition.

Things were looking dire. Ellroy realized the math of the battle was going against him, unless something happened to change the situation quickly.

It was then that Herman Sikes returned to the fight with dozens of heavily armed men and women he had collected from all the remaining guard posts throughout the building. They were ready to fight and each one took up a position in front of Ellroy's exhausted people and let go with a barrage of slugs that hit the zombies like a hammer, pounding them, cutting them to pieces.

One of the new guys even had an old Thompson sub-machine gun. God alone knew where he found that but he was putting it to excellent use and it was helping turn the tide of battle with its incredible firepower. These were fresh shooters, raring to get into the battle. They had plenty of ammo and they were itching to use it on the zombies and rack up some kills.

They did.

"Spread out!" Ellroy ordered the newcomers. "You new people, share your ammo. Some of us are running low."

"I need .38 slugs here!" one woman repeated her plea of moments earlier.

Others chimed in with their needs and those needs were quickly met.

One of the new people, a young gal and a farmer's daughter from the bayou, passed the woman an extra box of .38 slugs. She never knew it but that gal had just won herself a friend for life if she could get a look at the relief on that woman's face.

More shots rang out. More zombies entered the gym at the wall opening, shambling in semi-slow motion, but now they seemed to be coming in sparse groupings. There were definitely fewer of them now. Most of the undead were torn up bad, down on the floor, motionless or struggling to revive. Many had lost arms or legs, so they were not as dangerous as they had been earlier; some were just crawling across the floor when they were shot full of lead.

Ellroy watched carefully, nodding with relief as the vile things were being hit again and again, going down more often. A spark of hope was growing in his heart. Maybe their breaking into the gym like this was the best thing after all? At least they were all located here in one place. Now they could all be got at and killed. If that was possible, it would offer some hope that his defenders could win the battle here.

It seemed all the zombies were here except the LaRontue brothers, the original and first zombie-things that had started this all. Where were they? Ellroy had been watching for them but as yet he had not spotted their filthy carcasses.

Then he saw them!

There they were!

Amos and Lamont LaRontue were now crawling through the opening to get into the gymnasium. Ellroy raised his pump shotgun, pointed it directly at them and then blasted the two dead things to hell, one shot after the other. The dead husks fell to the floor lifeless, blown into various large and small chunky pieces of rotten dried flesh and bone.

"Good riddance, you bastards!"

Ellroy was elated to see that zombies, and zombie leftover parts, were being shot at from all quarters and dropping down dead all around him. Soon more were dead than alive — or more accurately — more were down motionless than standing and attacking. The defenders still kept up their furious gunfire to be sure they filled every twitching piece of dead matter with lead slugs that tore it apart.

Ellroy now ordered the people who made up the defensive arc to move in, so the men and women stepped forward a few feet closer to the things, step by step to close the gap as they continued shooting. They kept up their wild fusillade of gunfire as they moved in ever closer and the effect on the zombie things was devastating.

There were definitely more of the invaders down and motionless now than up and attacking. That was good to see. But not all of them were down and out, most were eventually coming back to life, and seemed to be doing so more quickly now than Ellroy had ever seen them do before. Still and all, the sheriff felt a brief surge of hope now, and he could see it mirrored in the faces of the shooters and those huddled in fear behind the defensive arc of the perimeter created by their weapons. He realized that the living could still win this battle, if they acted fast.

"Herman!" Ellroy ordered his deputy. "Take five men and get those cans of gasoline from the storage room. Get them all, and bring them here now!"

Sikes picked his five men from the group and was soon away on his mission. Others took up their places in the line and kept up the fusillade of shots.

"Shoot them down!" Ellroy shouted, stoking up the defenders in an effort to get every last bit of energy and fight out of them. He knew they were dead tired, ready to drop from exhaustion, but there was no recourse, they had to fight or die. They only had fear and adrenalin keeping them going now. "We have them on the run! They're almost done. We almost got them!"

And they did have them almost done.

The undead things were badly shot up now, most were down on the floor motionless. Others were crawling around, partial bodies, moving torsos without legs, or headless things wriggling around in confusion. Severed legs wiggled obscenely trying to advance, while severed arms used grasping fingers to crawl across the floor and continue their attack in vain. These were all reanimated and still could be dangerous so the shooters kept pumping rounds into these bodies and body parts. The mayhem was terrific, maddening. The blood and smell was atrocious, some of the shooters were gagging. Most had no time to be sick. They were just too terrified. The sight was horrible, but to Sheriff Birch Ellroy and most of his shooters, it was, in a way, simply lovely. It was a sheer relief to see they were now winning.

The last zombie-thing was shot and went down dead to the gym floor at precisely 5:45 A.M.

It was already the next morning. The sun was coming up on a new day. What a night it had been, but Sheriff Birch Ellroy knew the job was not over yet.

"Quickly now! Before they reanimate," Ellroy ordered sharply. "Open that door to the baseball field. You men, start carrying the corpses and all the pieces of them outside. Don't miss anything. We'll make a pile of them in the center of the field and then burn them all."

The padlocks were unlocked, the outside door was flung open wide. A careful investigation found there were no more zombies outside to ambush them. They made sure the place was all clear.

Men and women put down their weapons and began the dirty but necessary task of removing the zombie bodies, and all the various body parts. It was a disgusting job. Every so often a gun went off when someone noticed a zombie coming back to life.

Deputy Herman Sikes and his people soon arrived with twenty five-gallon cans of gasoline.

"Take it outside, Herman, and dowse those damn corpses good. We're going to have a zombie roast!"

"About time!" Sikes shouted in gleeful relief. "Come on boys, you heard the sheriff."

Ellroy went over to Mychal Elkins and Quan See-Lo. "I want you guys to watch them bodies closely. You see so much as a finger or a toe twitch, I want you to blast it. I don't want anyone carrying one of those things over to the burn pile to be bit or scratched if one of those things suddenly wakes up."

"You got it, Sheriff," Elkins said, and he left with Quan.

Trudy Nelson came over. "There turned out to be way more than a hundred of them, Birch. More like two hundred of the things."

"Yeah, I think so," he said grimly. He hadn't had time to count them. They'd lost a lot of good people, they'd lost neighbors and friends, and family too. "I guess we should count them all, identify the bodies but ... "

"No," Doctor Carter added hastily as he came over. "Just do them all now. Burn them quick, Birch. Right away."

"I think that'd be best too," Trudy agreed with a deep sigh of regret. She knew for many people of the village there would never be any closure for what had happened to those they loved here tonight, but the danger was just too great to delay. The things had to be destroyed right away.

Sheriff Ellroy nodded, looked at the doctor, "You look like you want to say something, Howie?"

"I've been treating the wounded. We've got a good dozen that were scratched, clawed, or bit by the zombies when they first broke in here. Some of them have fevers already."

"Any chance of a recovery for any of them?"

"None, I'm afraid," the doc replied tersely, a hopeless sad look overcoming his features.

Ellroy knew what that meant. More victims. More zombies. They'd all go the way Jake's two sons had gone. So be it. "Make them comfortable. Do what you can for them. As soon as they pass, I want their bodies set afire."

Doctor Carter nodded. "I see they're taking out the LaRontue brothers now. Maybe there'll be a special place in hell for those two."

"One can only hope," Trudy Nelson added softly.

"I for one don't blame them for what they did but I would like to know just how this all got started," Sheriff Ellroy told them as he looked at the devastation that surrounded him. His beautiful small town jurisdiction, Macedonia Parish, was in ruins. Somewhere, over 200 of his people were dead; men, women and children. Probably more once it all got sorted out in the days to come. Families were destroyed, the inhabitants of the parish were traumatized and terrorized beyond anything they'd ever seen or lived through. Nothing, not World War II, not Vietnam, not even Katrina, could compare to this nightmare.

Ellroy watched as the bodies were carried out of the gym quickly and placed into a large pile in the center of the baseball field behind the high school. Every once in a while a shot rang out, denoting a slug placed into the head or heart of a zombie as it attempted to reanimate itself, now made silent and motionless for a while — until it tried to reanimate itself once again.

Ellroy shuddered, hopefully soon the creatures would all be collected and burned. He watched grimly as what had once been the LaRontue brothers were taken out and thrown onto the pile of corpses. They now lay motionless up at the top of that mass of undead flesh.

Deputy Sikes and his men were dousing the pile with can after can of gasoline. These were dozens of heavy five and ten-gallon cans. They emptied the large cans, spreading the accelerant liberally. They'd gone back once already for more cans of gas and now Ellroy was amazed to see a huge Exxon gas truck pulling up behind the school building.

"Reinforcements, Birch," Sikes told the sheriff with a grin.

The driver, Sammy Palermo, got out of his gas truck and opened up the hose to spew the mound of zombie remains totally soaking them in gasoline. "This should do the trick, Birch."

"Good, Sammy," Ellroy said simply.

When all the undead remains had been collected and thrown on the pile, and the gasoline had been allowed a few minutes to soak into the pile good and deep, a flame was lit. All the survivors of the siege at the high school crowded around as the bodies were set afire in a torrential blaze that lit up the early morning sky for miles.

No one cheered, few even cried yet. They just stood frozen and watched, each survivor alone with their own thoughts, their own nightmares that would be with them for the rest of their lives.

"It's a new day, Birch," Susan Ellroy told her husband with a small sad smile. She stood beside Birch, her little hand grasping his firmly as their son Tommy hugged them.

Sheriff Birch Ellroy sighed heavily and hugged his wife and son to him in a firm embrace. They'd pulled through, they'd made it alive and safe. Of course he was happy about that, joyful even, but the revelation was bittersweet when he looked at the faces of all the people around them—friends and neighbors all who were missing family members. Many of those missing family members were now burning brightly in the massive bonfire before them.

A funeral pyre for all the dead and undead.

Now there were tears, then cries of sadness and rage. There were recriminations of all kinds and many questions asked. How could this have happened? Why did it happen here? Why my son, or daughter? Why my mother or brother?

Sheriff Birch Ellroy was just a simple man but he began to wonder about it too as the day wore on and the massive fire burned itself long and fast. Hours later it finally went out to leave behind a warm heap of bright embers and dark smoky ashes.

The survivors sighed in relief: the zombie threat was over. Or so they hoped. So too hoped Sheriff Ellroy, but he was taking nothing for granted. He sent out armed patrols all throughout the parish. Hours later there were no reports of any undead sightings, no more attacks.

Chapter 22: The Witch Woman

 **HE** NEXT DAY Sheriff Birch Ellroy and his deputy, Herman Sikes took a ride out to the spot below Spring Bridge where the two cars containing the State Troopers and FBI agents had fallen into the ravine and burst into flames.

"It's around here where I saw the cars, Birch," Sikes said leading the sheriff through rough brambles and thickets over to where they came upon a large burnt patch of ground with the husks of two burnt-out automobiles in the center.

"That's them there," Sikes said softly. "Hey, look, there's someone there."

Ellroy strained his eyes to discover that it was a woman, a very old woman. He and his deputy silently walked closer, watching her carefully.

"It's that Sabella! The gypsy witch-woman," Sikes whispered nervously. He'd heard all about her and drew his weapon. "What's she doing, Birch?"

Damned if he knew. Ellroy stood motionless, shocked and surprised by the appearance of the old crone. "Witch" seemed an accurate word for her, and while the sheriff didn't believe in such things—then again until a week ago he hadn't believed in zombies either!—she sure did look like a witch to him. And she was so old now! What the hell had happened to her? She had been young and lovely once—and not so long ago either! The sheriff knew that she was thought by everyone in his parish to be a very wicked witch. Now what the hell was she doing?

Ellroy and Sikes didn't say a word as they moved closer, watching the strange woman. She hardly seemed to notice the two men so involved was she in what she was doing—standing before the burnt state police vehicles, chanting wildly in an unknown tone, cackling insanely, making bizarre geometric gestures with her fingers in the air before her like it was some insane form of satanic sign language.

"Black magic!" Sikes blurted in a fearful whisper to the man at his side. He grasped the handle of his .38 Police Special tighter than ever.

"Be quiet," Ellroy ordered softly, still watching the woman, fascinated by her and by what she was doing. What was she doing? Why was she out here? This was the ass middle of nowhere. What was she trying to do with those two cars—or was it the lifeless bodies inside the cars?

A cold chill came over Ellroy, his head started pounding again with the resurgence of a headache he'd not had for a day or so. Now it was back full force as he watched that old crone, that witch-woman known as Sabella. What was that crazy old woman trying to do? Bring back the dead?

Ellroy shuddered with the cold chill of impending doom. Maybe that's just what she was trying to do. But could it be? How could she do that?

He watched in awe as Sabella continued spouting her bizarre words, harsh chants; her wild gyrations and gestures made in slow motion like some freakish death dancer.

Necromancer?

Suddenly the creaking sound from an opening door of one of the autos got Ellroy's attention. He spotted a dead burnt hand pushing the door open. It was movement inside where there should be no movement—accompanied by a wild cackle of insane glee from the old crone in front of him.

"Awaken my children!" the old woman's voice chanted, the only words she had spoken in a language that either of the men could understand in all her strange sounds.

Ellroy watched in amazement and his deputy stood by frozen in terror at what they were seeing. Was this actually happening? Was Sabella somehow bringing these dead men back to life? If so, why? For what reason?

Ellroy looked to the face of his deputy, the man was ashen and clearly terrified.

Was this happening all over again?

Oh no, not on his watch!

Ellroy starred at the old woman in total fascination, she was clearly an insane mental case, and yet … He now noticed the growing movement inside the car, and finally he realized the truth. It was not only happening all over again, this is the way that it had originally begun. She had caused it all. Somehow. In some way he could not understand and maybe could never understand. It had all been due to this old witch-woman. It had all been Sabella's doing!

Sheriff Birch Ellroy took the safety off his .45 and then called out to the woman.

"Sabella! Stop it now!"

The old crone suddenly turned and looked upon the sheriff. Her eyes blazed fire red with intense hate.

"You have come to stop Sabella. No one stops Sabella. My magic is strong. My rage is endless. My revenge is sweet. Arise my children! Arise and feast upon these two who would mock me!" she cried these words to the burnt corpses inside the two vehicles and amazingly they answered her with slow but definite movement.

Suddenly the doors on both cars sprung open and the dead things inside—the rotted dead bodies of six Louisiana State Police and two New Orleans FBI agents—slowly twitched and shook with renewed life.

"God damn this!" Ellroy shouted in rage. He let loose with two rapid shots to the witch-woman's head that smashed her skull and killed her instantly. The old crone fell to the ground without a sound.

`'"Herman? Herman, wake up, man! Come out of it! Help me kill these bastards one more time, then we'll set them all ablaze."

"The old woman too?" Sikes asked as he came back to reality and began shooting the slowly moving corpses. The zombies, which had not fully reanimated yet, proved easy targets for the sheriff and his deputy now that the witch-woman was dead.

"Yes, especially that woman!" Ellroy barked now, not willing to take any chances.

The fusillade of shots from the two men rained down into the corpses and the old woman in a tearing, searing burst of mayhem. It was over quickly, the eight bodies were taken out and placed in a pile. Sabella, too, was added to the top of that pile and then all were doused with gasoline and set ablaze.

"And that, I hope, is the end of zombies in Macedonia Parish," Sheriff Birch Ellroy stated grimly.

"Amen to that," Deputy Sikes added in relief.

Chapter 23: All Is Explained

**HE** STATE POLICE and the media came into Macedonia Parish in a long vehicle convoy the day after next. They were joined by the FBI. They all began their investigation for the missing serial killer. They hardly took to heart what the local sheriff and the local villagers told them about some wild story concerning zombies. Even though the local doctor backed up the story — but, after all, he was just a rural GP — not any kind of medical specialist. He hadn't even graduated from the proper medical schools — those elite schools where the leaders who would become movers and shakers in our nation sprouted from like evil, rancid flowers. He was a no one. They were all no ones here — but of course none of the outsiders ever said that publicly.

It was eventually decided that the entire village needed a good supply of competent shrinks and a lot of very strong psychotropic medical prescriptions.

The State guys eventually did discover that it seemed that a lot of the people in the parish had gone missing. Or they had simply left town? They put the reason for that to some being killed by the serial killer, while others left the parish out of fear. Or shame. It made sense they'd leave with a killer on the lose, and it was assumed they'd all return once the State Police and the FBI had things under control again. Just like the people had left after Katrina. Many left, some never came back. Some moved to Texas, or other places. That made a lot more sense than some crazy explanation about zombies.

Nevertheless, the facts had to be faced that something horrific had happened in Macedonia Parish and there was no real evidence of any serial killer. That made things a bit difficult for the State Police and FBI boys to explain. Forensics found various burn sites throughout the village. The largest of these was right outside the wreckage of what was left of the local high school. Out on the baseball field. Officials from outside the parish seemed to think some kind of riot had taken place at the high school, probably over some sporting event? A basketball game in the gym, that perhaps had got out of hand? They all agreed that even though there were no games on the schedule, it must be something like that. After all, what else could it be?

That zombie theory was discounted right away. It was ridiculous. It was nothing any of these so finely educated all-knowing experts took seriously at all. After all, they were the elite, they knew all the answers, and they had serious careers to consider. Zombies just did not just mix with politics and promotions, big juicy research grants and lifetime tenure. Zombies were a career killer for these folks.

However, those burn spots did trouble some experts. Some explanation was needed for that. It was believed that just one of the burn spots alone could have contained as many as two hundred bodies. Maybe more. The locals said they were the missing people of Macedonia Parish. That's what every one of the local inhabitants told the FBI. They all told the same zombie story, too, but the experts from New Orleans just couldn't buy that bit of craziness. It just couldn't be true after all. It had to be something else, some rational explanation—this zombie fantasy was just some form of mass hallucination due to trauma, surely. Trauma due to the serial killer, or mass murderer … or whatever …

The experts decided the burn spot was most probably the remains of some huge barbecue pit for a basketball or football game celebration at the high school. The remains were indeterminate, so intense had been the fire, that while remains might be human, they could just as easily be from pigs. DNA tests were inconclusive. The remains could be from nothing more ominous than some huge high school pig roast. Anyway, it fit the sports celebration theory. All the destruction at the high school could have been from an after game riot. At least, that made a lot more sense than zombies! Anything made more sense than zombies!

Officials and experts from outside the parish, from the State Police and from the FBI, investigated day and night, they talked to the locals again, they taped interviews, they took sworn depositions. They got the entire zombie story first-hand from the survivors.

They didn't believe one word of it.

They left the village sure that the entire population of Macedonia Parish was suffering from some form of mass psychosis. In the end, the entire population of Macedonia Parish was glad to see them go. People knew what they had seen, they knew what they had lived through. Now they just wanted get back to business and rebuild their lives.

No one much talks about what happened that week in the summer of a certain year in Macedonia Parish these days. Locals don't like to relive any of it and they never discuss it with outsiders.

Sheriff Birch Ellroy is still in office, reelected unanimously. He runs a series of strict neighborhood watches now that include every able-bodied man and woman in the parish. Everyone is involved in it. All are thoroughly armed. They jokingly call it the zombie patrol.

But it's no joke to them.

LaRontue Mansion is still there too. Old and weathered, the paint peeled, vines growing up all around it and even into it. They say in the village that with the death of Amos and Lamont LaRontue the house has now fallen to some wayward niece up in New York City. It is said she might be coming down to the parish for a visit and to claim her inheritance, but no one has showed up yet and the parish is not partial to outsiders.

It is said by some that the shade of the old witch-woman Sabella still haunts LaRontue Mansion. It is said by some that she shall rise again some day and take her revenge once more.

THE END

GARY LOVISI is a Mystery Writers of America Edgar Nominated author for his Sherlock Holmes pastiche, "The Adventure of the Missing Detective." His latest books are *Sherlock Holmes: The Baron's Revenge* (Airship27 Productions, 2012, tpb, $15); *Mars Needs Books* (Wildside Press) a science fiction novel; *Bad Girls Need Love Too*, a lovely gift book full of sexy pulp fiction paperback cover art (Krause, hc, 2011, $12.99) and the edited anthology, *Battling Boxing Stories* (Wildside Press, 2012, tpb, $20). Lovisi is also the founder of Gryphon Books, editor of *Paperback Parade* and *Hardboiled* magazines, and sponsors an annual book collectors show in New York City that just celebrated its 25th year. To find out more about him, his work, or Gryphon Books, visit his web site at:

www.gryphonbooks.com

ED COUTTS was born and raised in New York City's Hell's Kitchen and started drawing at the age of 5. Current projects include painted covers and interior illustrations for PulpAdventure's "Hellfire Lounge" anthology series, and Dark Quest's "Bad-Ass Faerie Tales" and "Gaslight and Grimm." Working in pencil, ink and paint, comic book credits include AC Comics, Kaso Comics, Three J Productions, and Palisades Press. He has produced hundreds of portraits for "Character Counts," several posters for off-Broadway plays, and cards for "Sadlittles." Visit his web site at:

www.edcouttsart.com

GAVIN L. O'KEEFE was born in Melbourne, Australia, and currently lives in South Berwick, Maine. His illustrations have been published internationally in numerous books, magazines and other media. He recently released his new illustrated version of L. Frank Baum's *The Wonderful Wizard of Oz* (Ramble House), interpreted along Theosophical lines. He continues to design covers and create art for books for the Ramble House / Surinam Turtle Press / Dancing Tuatara Press conglomerate. Visit his web site at:

www.gavinokeefe.com

RAMBLE HOUSE's
HARRY STEPHEN KEELER WEBWORK MYSTERIES
(RH) indicates the title is available ONLY in the RAMBLE HOUSE edition

The Ace of Spades Murder
The Affair of the Bottled Deuce (RH)
The Amazing Web
The Barking Clock
Behind That Mask
The Book with the Orange Leaves
The Bottle with the Green Wax Seal
The Box from Japan
The Case of the Canny Killer
The Case of the Crazy Corpse (RH)
The Case of the Flying Hands (RH)
The Case of the Ivory Arrow
The Case of the Jeweled Ragpicker
The Case of the Lavender Gripsack
The Case of the Mysterious Moll
The Case of the 16 Beans
The Case of the Transparent Nude (RH)
The Case of the Transposed Legs
The Case of the Two-Headed Idiot (RH)
The Case of the Two Strange Ladies
The Circus Stealers (RH)
Cleopatra's Tears
A Copy of Beowulf (RH)
The Crimson Cube (RH)
The Face of the Man From Saturn
Find the Clock
The Five Silver Buddhas
The 4th King
The Gallows Waits, My Lord! (RH)
The Green Jade Hand
Finger! Finger!
Hangman's Nights (RH)
I, Chameleon (RH)
I Killed Lincoln at 10:13! (RH)
The Iron Ring
The Man Who Changed His Skin (RH)
The Man with the Crimson Box
The Man with the Magic Eardrums
The Man with the Wooden Spectacles
The Marceau Case
The Matilda Hunter Murder

The Monocled Monster
The Murder of London Lew
The Murdered Mathematician
The Mysterious Card (RH)
The Mysterious Ivory Ball of Wong Shing Li (RH)
The Mystery of the Fiddling Cracksman
The Peacock Fan
The Photo of Lady X (RH)
The Portrait of Jirjohn Cobb
Report on Vanessa Hewstone (RH)
Riddle of the Travelling Skull
Riddle of the Wooden Parrakeet (RH)
The Scarlet Mummy (RH)
The Search for X-Y-Z
The Sharkskin Book
Sing Sing Nights
The Six From Nowhere (RH)
The Skull of the Waltzing Clown
The Spectacles of Mr. Cagliostro
Stand By—London Calling!
The Steeltown Strangler
The Stolen Gravestone (RH)
Strange Journey (RH)
The Strange Will
The Straw Hat Murders (RH)
The Street of 1000 Eyes (RH)
Thieves' Nights
Three Novellos (RH)
The Tiger Snake
The Trap (RH)
Vagabond Nights (Defrauded Yeggman)
Vagabond Nights 2 (10 Hours)
The Vanishing Gold Truck
The Voice of the Seven Sparrows
The Washington Square Enigma
When Thief Meets Thief
The White Circle (RH)
The Wonderful Scheme of Mr. Christopher Thorne
X. Jones—of Scotland Yard
Y. Cheung, Business Detective

Keeler Related Works

A To Izzard: A Harry Stephen Keeler Companion by Fender Tucker — Articles and stories about Harry, by Harry, and in his style. Included is a compleat bibliography.

Wild About Harry: Reviews of Keeler Novels — Edited by Richard Polt & Fender Tucker — 22 reviews of works by Harry Stephen Keeler from *Keeler News*. A perfect introduction to the author.

The Keeler Keyhole Collection: Annotated newsletter rants from Harry Stephen Keeler, edited by Francis M. Nevins. Over 400 pages of incredibly personal Keeleriana.

Fakealoo — Pastiches of the style of Harry Stephen Keeler by selected demented members of the HSK Society. Updated every year with the new winner.

Strands of the Web: Short Stories of Harry Stephen Keeler — 29 stories, just about all that Keeler wrote, are edited and introduced by Fred Cleaver.

RAMBLE HOUSE's Loon Sanctuary

A Clear Path to Cross — Sharon Knowles short mystery stories by Ed Lynskey.

A Jimmy Starr Omnibus — Three 40s novels by Jimmy Starr.

A Niche in Time and Other Stories — Classic SF by William F. Temple

A Roland Daniel Double: The Signal and The Return of Wu Fang — Classic thrillers from the 30s.

A Shot Rang Out — Three decades of reviews and articles by today's Anthony Boucher, Jon Breen. An essential book for any mystery lover's library.

A Smell of Smoke — A 1951 English countryside thriller by Miles Burton.

A Snark Selection — Lewis Carroll's *The Hunting of the Snark* with two Snarkian chapters by Harry Stephen Keeler — Illustrated by Gavin L. O'Keefe.

A Young Man's Heart — A forgotten early classic by Cornell Woolrich.

Alexander Laing Novels — *The Motives of Nicholas Holtz* and *Dr. Scarlett*, stories of medical mayhem and intrigue from the 30s.

An Angel in the Street — Modern hardboiled noir by Peter Genovese.

Automaton — Brilliant treatise on robotics: 1928-style! By H. Stafford Hatfield.

Away From the Here and Now — Clare Winger Harris stories, collected by Richard A. Lupoff.

Beast or Man? — A 1930 novel of racism and horror by Sean M'Guire. Introduced by John Pelan.

Black Hogan Strikes Again — Australia's Peter Renwick pens a tale of the 30s outback.

Black River Falls — Suspense from the master, Ed Gorman.

Blondy's Boy Friend — A snappy 1930 story by Philip Wylie, writing as Leatrice Homesley.

Blood in a Snap — The *Finnegan's Wake* of the 21st century, by Jim Weiler.

Blood Moon — The first of the Robert Payne series by Ed Gorman.

Bogart '48 — Hollywood action with Bogie by John Stanley and Kenn Davis.

Calling Lou Largo! — Two Lou Largo novels by William Ard.

Cornucopia of Crime — Francis M. Nevins assembled this huge collection of his writings about crime literature and the people who write it. Essential for any serious mystery library.

Corpse Without Flesh — Strange novel of forensics by George Bruce.

Crimson Clown Novels — By Johnston McCulley, author of the Zorro novels, *The Crimson Clown* and *The Crimson Clown Again*.

Dago Red — 22 tales of dark suspense by Bill Pronzini.

Dark Sanctuary — Weird Menace story by H. B. Gregory

David Hume Novels — *Corpses Never Argue, Cemetery First Stop, Make Way for the Mourners, Eternity Here I Come*. 1930s British hardboiled fiction with an attitude.

Dead Man Talks Too Much — Hollywood boozer by Weed Dickenson.

Death Leaves No Card — One of the most unusual murdered-in-the-tub mysteries you'll ever read. By Miles Burton.

Death March of the Dancing Dolls and Other Stories — Volume Three in the Day Keene in the Detective Pulps series. Introduced by Bill Crider.

Deep Space and other Stories — A collection of SF gems by Richard A. Lupoff.

Detective Duff Unravels It — Episodic mysteries by Harvey O'Higgins.

Diabolic Candelabra — Classic 30s mystery by E.R. Punshon.

Dime Novels: Ramble House's 10-Cent Books — *Knife in the Dark* by Robert Leslie Bellem, *Hot Lead* and *Song of Death* by Ed Earl Repp, *A Hashish House in New York* by H.H. Kane, and five more.

Don Diablo: Book of a Lost Film — Two-volume treatment of a western by Paul Landres, with diagrams. Intro by Francis M. Nevins.

Dope and Swastikas — Two strange novels from 1922 by Edmund Snell

Dope Tales #1 — Two dope-riddled classics; *Dope Runners* by Gerald Grantham and *Death Takes the Joystick* by Phillip Condé.

Dope Tales #2 — Two more narco-classics; *The Invisible Hand* by Rex Dark and *The Smokers of Hashish* by Norman Berrow.

Dope Tales #3 — Two enchanting novels of opium by the master, Sax Rohmer. *Dope* and *The Yellow Claw*.

Double Hot — Two 60s softcore sex novels by Morris Hershman.

Dr. Odin — Douglas Newton's 1933 racial potboiler comes back to life.

Evangelical Cockroach — Jack Woodford writes about writing.

Evidence in Blue — 1938 mystery by E. Charles Vivian.

Fatal Accident — Murder by automobile, a 1936 mystery by Cecil M. Wills.

Fighting Mad — Todd Robbins' 1922 novel about boxing and life

Finger-prints Never Lie — A 1939 classic detective novel by John G. Brandon.

Freaks and Fantasies — Eerie tales by Tod Robbins, collaborator of Tod Browning on the film FREAKS.

Gadsby — A lipogram (a novel without the letter E). Ernest Vincent Wright's last work, published in 1939 right before his death.

Gelett Burgess Novels — *The Master of Mysteries, The White Cat, Two O'Clock Courage, Ladies in Boxes, Find the Woman, The Heart Line, The Picaroons* and *Lady Mechante*. Recently added is A Gelett Burgess Sampler, edited by Alfred Jan. All are introduced by Richard A. Lupoff.

Geronimo — S. M. Barrett's 1905 autobiography of a noble American.

Hake Talbot Novels — *Rim of the Pit, The Hangman's Handyman*. Classic locked room mysteries, with mapback covers by Gavin O'Keefe.

Hands Out of Hell and Other Stories — John H. Knox's eerie hallucinations

Hell is a City — William Ard's masterpiece.

Hollywood Dreams — A novel of Tinsel Town and the Depression by Richard O'Brien.

Hostesses in Hell and Other Stories — Russell Gray's most graphic stories

House of the Restless Dead — Strange and ominous tales by Hugh B. Cave

I Stole $16,000,000 — A true story by cracksman Herbert E. Wilson.

Inclination to Murder — 1966 thriller by New Zealand's Harriet Hunter.

Invaders from the Dark — Classic werewolf tale from Greye La Spina.

J. Poindexter, Colored — Classic satirical black novel by Irvin S. Cobb.

Jack Mann Novels — Strange murder in the English countryside. *Gees' First Case, Nightmare Farm, Grey Shapes, The Ninth Life, The Glass Too Many, Her Ways Are Death, The Kleinert Case* and *Maker of Shadows*.

Jake Hardy — A lusty western tale from Wesley Tallant.

Jim Harmon Double Novels — *Vixen Hollow/Celluloid Scandal, The Man Who Made Maniacs/Silent Siren, Ape Rape/Wanton Witch, Sex Burns Like Fire/Twist Session, Sudden Lust/Passion Strip, Sin Unlimited/Harlot Master, Twilight Girls/Sex Institution*. Written in the early 60s and never reprinted until now.

Joel Townsley Rogers Novels and Short Stories — By the author of *The Red Right Hand: Once In a Red Moon, Lady With the Dice, The Stopped Clock, Never Leave My Bed*. Also two short story collections: *Night of Horror* and *Killing Time*.

John Carstairs, Space Detective — Arboreal Sci-fi by Frank Belknap Long

Joseph Shallit Novels — *The Case of the Billion Dollar Body, Lady Don't Die on My Doorstep, Kiss the Killer, Yell Bloody Murder, Take Your Last Look*. One of America's best 50's authors and a favorite of author Bill Pronzini.

Keller Memento — 45 short stories of the amazing and weird by Dr. David Keller.

Killer's Caress — Cary Moran's 1936 hardboiled thriller.

Lady of the Yellow Death and Other Stories — More stories by Wyatt Blassingame.

League of the Grateful Dead and Other Stories — Volume One in the Day Keene in the Detective Pulps series.

Library of Death — Ghastly tale by Ronald S. L. Harding, introduced by John Pelan

Malcolm Jameson Novels and Short Stories — *Astonishing! Astounding!, Tarnished Bomb, The Alien Envoy and Other Stories* and *The Chariots of San Fernando and Other Stories*. All introduced and edited by John Pelan or Richard A. Lupoff.

Man Out of Hell and Other Stories — Volume II of the John H. Knox weird pulps collection.

Marblehead: A Novel of H.P. Lovecraft — A long-lost masterpiece from Richard A. Lupoff. This is the "director's cut", the long version that has never been published before.

Master of Souls — Mark Hansom's 1937 shocker is introduced by weirdologist John Pelan.

Max Afford Novels — *Owl of Darkness, Death's Mannikins, Blood on His Hands, The Dead Are Blind, The Sheep and the Wolves, Sinners in Paradise* and *Two Locked Room Mysteries and a Ripping Yarn* by one of Australia's finest mystery novelists.

Money Brawl — Two books about the writing business by Jack Woodford and H. Bedford-Jones. Introduced by Richard A. Lupoff.

More Secret Adventures of Sherlock Holmes — Gary Lovisi's second collection of tales about the unknown sides of the great detective.

Muddled Mind: Complete Works of Ed Wood, Jr. — David Hayes and Hayden Davis deconstruct the life and works of the mad, but canny, genius.

Murder among the Nudists — A mystery from 1934 by Peter Hunt, featuring a naked Detective-Inspector going undercover in a nudist colony.

Murder in Black and White — 1931 classic tennis whodunit by Evelyn Elder.

Murder in Shawnee — Two novels of the Alleghenies by John Douglas: *Shawnee Alley Fire* and *Haunts.*

Murder in Silk — A 1937 Yellow Peril novel of the silk trade by Ralph Trevor.

My Deadly Angel — 1955 Cold War drama by John Chelton.

My First Time: The One Experience You Never Forget — Michael Birchwood — 64 true first-person narratives of how they lost it.

Mysterious Martin, the Master of Murder — Two versions of a strange 1912 novel by Tod Robbins about a man who writes books that can kill.

Norman Berrow Novels — *The Bishop's Sword, Ghost House, Don't Go Out After Dark, Claws of the Cougar, The Smokers of Hashish, The Secret Dancer, Don't Jump Mr. Boland!, The Footprints of Satan, Fingers for Ransom, The Three Tiers of Fantasy, The Spaniard's Thumb, The Eleventh Plague, Words Have Wings, One Thrilling Night, The Lady's in Danger, It Howls at Night, The Terror in the Fog, Oil Under the Window, Murder in the Melody, The Singing Room.* This is the complete Norman Berrow library of locked-room mysteries, several of which are masterpieces.

Old Faithful and Other Stories — SF classic tales by Raymond Z. Gallun

Old Times' Sake — Short stories by James Reasoner from Mike Shayne Magazine.

One Dreadful Night — A classic mystery by Ronald S. L. Harding

Pair O' Jacks — A mystery novel and a diatribe about publishing by Jack Woodford

Perfect .38 — Two early Timothy Dane novels by William Ard. More to come.

Prince Pax — Devilish intrigue by George Sylvester Viereck and Philip Eldridge

Prose Bowl — Futuristic satire of a world where hack writing has replaced football as our national obsession, by Bill Pronzini and Barry N. Malzberg.

Red Light — The history of legal prostitution in Shreveport Louisiana by Eric Brock. Includes wonderful photos of the houses and the ladies.

Researching American-Made Toy Soldiers — A 276-page collection of a lifetime of articles by toy soldier expert Richard O'Brien.

Reunion in Hell — Volume One of the John H. Knox series of weird stories from the pulps. Introduced by horror expert John Pelan.

Ripped from the Headlines! — The Jack the Ripper story as told in the newspaper articles in the *New York* and *London Times.*

Robert Randisi Novels — *No Exit to Brooklyn* and *The Dead of Brooklyn.* The first two Nick Delvecchio novels.

Rough Cut & New, Improved Murder — Ed Gorman's first two novels.

R.R. Ryan Novels — Freak Museum and The Subjugated Beast, two horror classics.

Ruled By Radio — 1925 futuristic novel by Robert L. Hadfield & Frank E. Farncombe.

Rupert Penny Novels — *Policeman's Holiday, Policeman's Evidence, Lucky Policeman, Policeman in Armour, Sealed Room Murder, Sweet Poison, The Talkative Policeman, She had to Have Gas* and *Cut and Run* (by Martin Tanner.) Rupert Penny is the pseudonym of Australian Charles Thornett, a master of the locked room, impossible crime plot.

Sacred Locomotive Flies — Richard A. Lupoff's psychedelic SF story.

Sam — Early gay novel by Lonnie Coleman.

Sand's Game — Spectacular hard-boiled noir from Ennis Willie, edited by Lynn Myers and Stephen Mertz, with contributions from Max Allan Collins, Bill Crider, Wayne Dundee, Bill Pronzini, Gary Lovisi and James Reasoner.

Sand's War — More violent fiction from the typewriter of Ennis Willie

Satan's Den Exposed — True crime in Truth or Consequences New Mexico — Award-winning journalism by the *Desert Journal.*

Satans of Saturn — Novellas from the pulps by Otis Adelbert Kline and E. H. Price

Satan's Sin House and Other Stories — Horrific gore by Wayne Rogers

Secrets of a Teenage Superhero — Graphic lit by Jonathan Sweet

Sex Slave — Potboiler of lust in the days of Cleopatra by Dion Leclerq, 1966.

Shadows' Edge — Two early novels by Wade Wright: *Shadows Don't Bleed* and *The Sharp Edge*.

Sideslip — 1968 SF masterpiece by Ted White and Dave Van Arnam.

Slammer Days — Two full-length prison memoirs: *Men into Beasts* (1952) by George Sylvester Viereck and *Home Away From Home* (1962) by Jack Woodford.

Slippery Staircase — 1930s whodunit from E.C.R. Lorac

Sorcerer's Chessmen — John Pelan introduces this 1939 classic by Mark Hansom.

Star Griffin — Michael Kurland's 1987 masterpiece of SF drollery is back.

Stakeout on Millennium Drive — Award-winning Indianapolis Noir by Ian Woollen.

Strands of the Web: Short Stories of Harry Stephen Keeler — Edited and Introduced by Fred Cleaver.

Summer Camp for Corpses and Other Stories — Weird Menace tales from Arthur Leo Zagat; introduced by John Pelan.

Suzy — A collection of comic strips by Richard O'Brien and Bob Vojtko from 1970.

Tales of the Macabre and Ordinary — Modern twisted horror by Chris Mikul, author of the *Bizarrism* series.

Tenebrae — Ernest G. Henham's 1898 horror tale brought back.

The Amorous Intrigues & Adventures of Aaron Burr — by Anonymous. Hot historical action about the man who almost became Emperor of Mexico.

The Anthony Boucher Chronicles — edited by Francis M. Nevins. Book reviews by Anthony Boucher written for the *San Francisco Chronicle*, 1942 – 1947. Essential and fascinating reading by the best book reviewer there ever was.

The Barclay Catalogs — Two essential books about toy soldier collecting by Richard O'Brien

The Basil Wells Omnibus — A collection of Wells' stories by Richard A. Lupoff

The Beautiful Dead and Other Stories — Dreadful tales from Donald Dale

The Best of 10-Story Book — edited by Chris Mikul, over 35 stories from the literary magazine Harry Stephen Keeler edited.

The Black Dark Murders — Vintage 50s college murder yarn by Milt Ozaki, writing as Robert O. Saber.

The Book of Time — The classic novel by H.G. Wells is joined by sequels by Wells himself and three stories by Richard A. Lupoff. Illustrated by Gavin L. O'Keefe.

The Case in the Clinic — One of E.C.R. Lorac's finest.

The Case of the Bearded Bride — #4 in the Day Keene in the Detective Pulps series

The Case of the Little Green Men — Mack Reynolds wrote this love song to sci-fi fans back in 1951 and it's now back in print.

The Case of the Withered Hand — 1936 potboiler by John G. Brandon.

The Charlie Chaplin Murder Mystery — A 2004 tribute by noted film scholar, Wes D. Gehring.

The Chinese Jar Mystery — Murder in the manor by John Stephen Strange, 1934.

The Compleat Calhoon — All of Fender Tucker's works: Includes *Totah Six-Pack, Weed, Women and Song* and *Tales from the Tower*, plus a CD of all of his songs.

The Compleat Ova Hamlet — Parodies of SF authors by Richard A. Lupoff. This is a brand new edition with more stories and more illustrations by Trina Robbins.

The Contested Earth and Other SF Stories — A never-before published space opera and seven short stories by Jim Harmon.

The Crimson Query — A 1929 thriller from Arlton Eadie. A perfect way to get introduced.

The Curse of Cantire — Classic 1939 novel of a family curse by Walter S. Masterman.

The Devil and the C.I.D. — Odd diabolic mystery by E.C.R. Lorac

The Devil Drives — An odd prison and lost treasure novel from 1932 by Virgil Markham.

The Devil's Mistress — A 1915 Scottish gothic tale by J. W. Brodie-Innes, a member of Aleister Crowley's Golden Dawn.

The Devil's Nightclub and Other Stories — John Pelan introduces some gruesome tales by Nat Schachner.

The Disentanglers — Episodic intrigue at the turn of last century by Andrew Lang

The Dumpling — Political murder from 1907 by Coulson Kernahan.

The End of It All and Other Stories — Ed Gorman selected his favorite short stories for this huge collection.

The Fangs of Suet Pudding — A 1944 novel of the German invasion by Adams Farr

The Ghost of Gaston Revere — From 1935, a novel of life and beyond by Mark Hansom, introduced by John Pelan.

The Girl in the Dark — A thriller from Roland Daniel

The Gold Star Line — Seaboard adventure from L.T. Reade and Robert Eustace.

The Golden Dagger — 1951 Scotland Yard yarn by E. R. Punshon.

The Great Orme Terror — Horror stories by Garnett Radcliffe from the pulps

The Hairbreadth Escapes of Major Mendax — Francis Blake Crofton's 1889 boys' book.

The House That Time Forgot and Other Stories — Insane pulpitude by Robert F. Young

The House of the Vampire — 1907 poetic thriller by George S. Viereck.

The Illustrious Corpse — Murder hijinx from Tiffany Thayer

The Incredible Adventures of Rowland Hern — Intriguing 1928 impossible crimes by Nicholas Olde.

The Julius Caesar Murder Case — A classic 1935 re-telling of the assassination by Wallace Irwin that's much more fun than the Shakespeare version.

The Koky Comics — A collection of all of the 1978-1981 Sunday and daily comic strips by Richard O'Brien and Mort Gerberg, in two volumes.

The Lady of the Terraces — 1925 missing race adventure by E. Charles Vivian.

The Lord of Terror — 1925 mystery with master-criminal, Fantômas.

The Melamare Mystery — A classic 1929 Arsene Lupin mystery by Maurice Leblanc

The Man Who Was Secrett — Epic SF stories from John Brunner

The Man Without a Planet — Science fiction tales by Richard Wilson

The N. R. De Mexico Novels — Robert Bragg, the real N.R. de Mexico, presents *Marijuana Girl, Madman on a Drum, Private Chauffeur* in one volume.

The Night Remembers — A 1991 Jack Walsh mystery from Ed Gorman.

The One After Snelling — Kickass modern noir from Richard O'Brien.

The Organ Reader — A huge compilation of just about everything published in the 1971-1972 radical bay-area newspaper, *THE ORGAN*. A coffee table book that points out the shallowness of the coffee table mindset.

The Poker Club — Three in one! Ed Gorman's ground-breaking novel, the short story it was based upon, and the screenplay of the film made from it.

The Private Journal & Diary of John H. Surratt — The memoirs of the man who conspired to assassinate President Lincoln.

The Secret Adventures of Sherlock Holmes — Three Sherlockian pastiches by the Brooklyn author/publisher, Gary Lovisi.

The Shadow on the House — Mark Hansom's 1934 masterpiece of horror is introduced by John Pelan.

The Sign of the Scorpion — A 1935 Edmund Snell tale of oriental evil.

The Singular Problem of the Stygian House-Boat — Two classic tales by John Kendrick Bangs about the denizens of Hades.

The Smiling Corpse — Philip Wylie and Bernard Bergman's odd 1935 novel.

The Spider: Satan's Murder Machines — A thesis about Iron Man

The Stench of Death: An Odoriferous Omnibus by Jack Moskovitz — Two complete novels and two novellas from 60's sleaze author, Jack Moskovitz.

The Story Writer and Other Stories — Classic SF from Richard Wilson

The Strange Case of the Antlered Man — 1935 dementia from Edwy Searles Brooks

The Strange Thirteen — Richard B. Gamon's odd stories about Raj India.

The Technique of the Mystery Story — Carolyn Wells' tips about writing.

The Threat of Nostalgia — A collection of his most obscure stories by Jon Breen

The Time Armada — Fox B. Holden's 1953 SF gem.

The Tongueless Horror and Other Stories — Volume One of the series of short stories from the weird pulps by Wyatt Blassingame.

The Tracer of Lost Persons — From 1906, an episodic novel that became a hit radio series in the 30s. Introduced by Richard A. Lupoff.

The Trail of the Cloven Hoof — Diabolical horror from 1935 by Arlton Eadie. Introduced by John Pelan.

The Triune Man — Mindscrambling science fiction from Richard A. Lupoff.

The Unholy Goddess and Other Stories — Wyatt Blassingame's first DTP compilation.

The Universal Holmes — Richard A. Lupoff's 2007 collection of five Holmesian pastiches and a recipe for giant rat stew.

RAMBLE HOUSE

Fender Tucker, Prop.   Gavin L. O'Keefe, Graphics

www.ramblehouse.com   fender@ramblehouse.com

228-826-1783   10329 Sheephead Drive, Vancleave MS 39565

www.ingramcontent.com/pod-product-compliance
Lightning Source LLC
Chambersburg PA
CBHW030331020726
47493CB00004B/1229